And On The Third Day

Stories

Derek O'Gorman

RIVERSONG
BOOKS

An Imprint of Sulis International Press
Los Angeles | Dallas | London

ISBN (print): 978-1-958139-53-0
ISBN (eBook): 978-1-958139-54-7

Published by Riversong Books
An Imprint of Sulis International
Los Angeles | Dallas | London

www.sulisinternational.com

Contents

Heroes

Dublin
April
1916

April 23rd

Harry had been uneasy as he cycled home through the city. It was nothing he could put his finger on, but more of a feeling, a sense that something was not quite right. Harry had a nose for that sort of thing. *Barbers' intuition* he liked to call it and that's all he ever wanted to do, cut hair. Saw an advert and answered it.

His wife Julia? Couldn't get her own head around it. "Barbering? For the Fifth Royal Dublin Fusiliers, the British…What will people think?"

"To hell with them," he had answered her that first morning, and as the days led to weeks her initial nervousness abated. The steady job brought a respectability, what they had strived for as a couple. And when baby Helen did arrive it gave them the leeway they needed with an extra mouth to feed.

*

Across town, Nora was beside herself with worry. All day her husband Donal had been gone again. He had taken to leaving their tenement lodgings, without any prior notice, for hours at a time these last few days to return in silence. It was behaviour that unnerved her and as she sat at the makeshift table in his absence this spring evening, she could feel the slight movements of their imminent new arrival. What should have been a glorious expectancy only added to her overwhelming sense of foreboding. She heard the familiar sound of the door closing softly.

"Is that you?" she called out, swallowing nervously, but her husband did not answer, choosing instead to enter the small, dimly lit kitchen in silence.

"You're back," she continued.

"I am," he finally spoke, removing his coat and throwing it across the timber table. He then went through the actions of surveying the room before he sat.

"And where have you been?" she asked tentatively.

"Out."

"I've been worried sick," she continued.

"Try not to be," he answered flatly.

"At my wit's end."

"I'll be fine Nora," he replied, this time raising his voice almost imperceptibly. "And anyway, it's not good for you, upsetting yourself. What did the nurse say?"

"You could have asked her yourself." Her voice was sharp. "She asked where you were. It's not right Donal, you out gallivanting God knows where, leaving me alone and a baby due at any minute."

Her husband stood from the table. "Don't be dramatic," he said, waving a hand dismissively as he crossed to the hearth. "We will have a cup of tea."

"Your solution to everything is tea!"

Donal ignored this latest barb from his expectant wife and worked in silence at the hearth.

"Days she said," Nora continued. "And I'm worried Donal. I don't know where you have been or what you are up to. I don't know what to make of it all."

Her husband crossed the floor in silence, moved his coat and set two large mugs down on the table before placing one gently in front of Nora. "Here, that will make you feel better," he said softly.

"It won't be much longer, Nora, love. Everything is changing for the better," he added reassuringly.

"Drink that down."

"So you keep telling me, Donal, but I don't see all this coming and going putting more food on the table."

"Jesus Nora!" he snapped back angrily. "I'm out there making a name for myself, doing this for us, and the baby."

Nora took a long slow sip from her mug. The black tea was lukewarm and bitter, but it seemed to galvanise her.

"Doing what exactly?"

"Don't Nora. You know I can't talk."

"You are gone all hours of the day, *for us*, but you can't tell me what it is you're up to. Not one crumb."

Donal slapped the palm of his hand firmly on the table, sending droplets of tea haphazardly across the uneven timber surface.

"No! I can't and that's the end of it!"

*

Julia need never worry, of that Harry was convinced. He didn't take risks, and he followed the same routine and route every morning. Before pointing his bike down Bishop's Street, he secured his clips, first right, then left, a jaunty wave to his wife and he was off.

"Be careful," she mouthed most mornings as he swung down the street, picking up a head of steam before gliding into Aungier Street. Once there he kept the bike at a steady pace, as he turned onto Dame Street before the final climb as he reached his destination. Dublin Castle, Cork Hill entrance. He always enjoyed that final ascent, and he would often allow his mind to wander then. Mostly it would be thoughts of Julia and their future together. He loved her dearly. He loved her dancing smile and how she threw her head back in laughter when he joked whether she was ever embarrassed for having married a barber.

"And a Fifth Royal Fusilier on top of that!" she often shot back.

The arrival of Helen completed them. Harry loved to arrive home and listen to Julia recount how they had spent their day together. Some evenings the child was still awake and Harry enjoyed taking the little one in his arms, but most times sleep had taken hold. On those occasions, he liked to sit beside the cot and watch his daughter sleep. This evening, it seemed to him that the innocent child was mirroring the restlessness of the city.

"Shh, don't wake her," Julia whispered, placing her hand on Harry's shoulder.

"It won't always be like this," he answered quietly.

Julia rubbed his shoulder softly. "You seem so certain of it," she said.

"There is talk at the barracks that the Western Front is starting to turn," Harry continued.

"Is that how you spend your day, talking about war?" Julia replied, taking a step back.

"Listening mostly love, and the word is that when that does happen, all the big cities will have work for those that served and like-minded men."

"Like-minded?"

"Yes, Julia, men of service."

"Even for the humble barbers?" she asked quizzically.

"Skilled men love, Birmingham, Liverpool, Manchester, take your pick."

"What are you talking about? Have you taken a fall off that old high nelly of yours, banged your crown?" Julia continued, playfully tapping the back of his head.

"Birmingham, love, a fresh start," Harry answered enthusiastically as he spun around to wheel Julia on to his lap.

"Will you stop Harry! The baby!" she laughed, offering little resistance.

"I'm serious love."

"Birmingham?"

"For starters."

"Liverpool?"

"For dessert. What do you think Julia love?"

*

Nora was determined, and no amount of table slapping or displaced tea was going to dissuade her.

"Is that all you have to say?" she replied firmly.

"Yes."

"You're a fool, Donal, a fool for yourself, always looking for something you can't have," she continued.

"I want something better, for the three of us, the family."

"And you think this charade is something that we need, something you won't even talk about with your own wife?"

Donal paused and took a long deliberate drink from his large mug before replacing it on the table. "I do, yes" he said matter-of-factly.

"You're living in a fantasy world Donal, and I'm not stupid, you know. Please listen to me. They will drop you like a hot spud." She was pleading now, and her words hung in the air of the dank kitchen.

"No, Nora, they are my comrades."

"Aren't we happy enough as we are?"

"You have to have ambition, that's all I'm saying."

Nora stood from the table and emptied the remnants of her tea into the hearth. The hissing filled the air. She was standing behind her husband now. "And skulking around street corners, that's ambition, is it?" Donal turned sharply to face her. "A small price to pay for Ireland. Would you prefer to go on living like this?" he barked. Nora stood motionless. "I'm going out," he added as he stood up roughly and grabbed his coat aggressively. Nora faced her husband squarely as he struggled into his coat. "Jesus Donal you can't keep running away!" she chided, but his momentum was now taking him out of the room.

"And I don't see any of your comrades offering you real work. Work that puts money in our pockets. Can they not do that for Ireland?"

Donal stopped abruptly.

"I have to prove myself first Nora. That's the way of it."

"Not to me," she replied forcefully as she stepped to the table and took Donal's mug back to the hearth. There she repeated the process of emptying out the dregs.

"When I have done that. Then it will be different. I promise."

Nora waited for the tea to burn off before speaking.

"Can you not just tell me the truth?"

"It's nothing to be worrying about. They just need me for a few days, that's all, and I don't want you to be fretting. And when it's done, if anyone comes asking, I was with you all day, the whole time. Will you do that for me?"

*

A fresh start, England. What did he want her to think?

"Birmingham?" the inaudibility of her own voice took her by surprise.

"A new beginning," Harry enthused as he kissed her. "Modest to begin with mind, but with hard work, who knows? In a year, a chain of barber shops across the city with twenty men, working for me, for us," his eyes danced with the intoxication of it all. "And you're good with numbers," he continued, "sensible, to keep the books balanced and an eye on things."

Julia felt powerless to contain her husband's wild abandon as he laid out his vision for their future, a version of her husband she had never known, until now.

"I have thought this through from every angle," Harry continued energetically.

"Twenty shops," she exhaled slowly.

"We can make it work, the three of us."

"Up sticks and leave."

"To make a proper life for ourselves and Helen. Just think of what it would be like."

Julia eased herself from his arms. She needed to stand, to unscramble her emotions, to diffuse Harry's exuberance.

"Well? Say something Julia."

"Yes," from where it had come from she did not know, hesitantly at first and then more confidently.

"Yes!"

"Yes?"

"Yes! Birmingham, Liverpool, Manchester, whatever it takes," Julia squealed with excitement and allowed herself to be swallowed into the arms of her husband once more.

*

Nora took a moment to process what she was hearing.

"So, you want me to lie."

"For God's sake Nora we are this close to putting the British in a spin," Donal cajoled.

"I won't do it."

"And you won't change your mind?"

"Jesus, Donal, can you not see sense for once in your life? You want to make a widow of me? Is that what you want?"

Donal advanced on her. "Keep your voice down, woman! You will get the whole place lifted."

"If that what it takes, to end this nonsense."

"Nonsense," gasped Donal, Nora's words stopping him in his tracks.

"Yes."

"You don't understand," Donal pleaded. "It's different this time. There is a plan in place, a proper plan."

"You're not listening to a word I'm saying. I married you because I believe in you, not some pie in the sky."

"Can you not do this one thing for me so? I'm not going to put us at risk, I give you my word."

Nora sat back to the table and Donal sat beside her taking her hands in his hands.

"They want me tomorrow, for a couple of hours, as a lookout, that's all."

"A lookout."

"Yes, just a couple of hours. God's honest truth, Nora, on the child's life."

"And after?" Nora asked.

"The people who stood up. They won't be forgotten. There will be positions to be filled."

"What kind of positions?"

"Military positions, in the new Republic."

"A Republic," Nora suppressed a dismissive laugh.

"A new Ireland, Nora, for the Irish people. A proper place to raise a child."

"I just want…the truth," Nora replied tiredly.

"Just a lookout, to keep an eye on things. In and out fast," Donal reassured, taking her in his arms. "Everything I do, every waking hour is for us love," Donal continued, kissing her softly. "That's all I'm interested in. I thought you'd be pleased, love, me doing my bit to give us a leg up. In and out fast. You won't even know I'm gone."

"Promise?"

"Yes, and if anyone asks, anyone at all, I was with you the whole day."

"A couple of hours and that's all?"

"Tops," Donal replied, kissing her again.

April 24th

"As I went down to a West Cork town"
  Known o'er sea and land

The soft lullaby never failed to ease Helen to sleep, and this morning Julia continued singing softly even though the child was now sound in her arms.

"Who should I meet but a maiden fair"
  Who took me by the hand

She stopped abruptly as Harry came to stand in the jamb of the door with his arms folded.

"Don't stop on my account," he encouraged. "You know I like to hear you sing the little one to sleep."

"Stop," his wife blushed as she continued to pace the room gently with their child.

"Go on. It's a day for a song, and you know it's a sweet voice you have," Harry continued.

"She led me dancing through fields of green"

Julia resumed self-consciously before stopping to stifle a laugh.

"She will have the voice of an angel someday, Julia love."

"And her father's looks."

"Finish it out, so and send me on my way to the barracks with a song in my heart and a spring in my step. Go on."

"We have had enough foolishness for one day," Julia said as she placed Helen into the cot. "And to be honest, it doesn't end well, an air my father taught me. He'd sing it to us when there was conflict in the house, to show the futility of it all."

"Did it work?"

"My father believed that blind faith, in anything, wasn't good. Told us that the ordinary men and women had to stick together."

"They were good, decent people," Harry agreed.

"They were."

"And they made good of what they had," Harry added. "And we must do the same, Julia. Will you finish it when I get home, so?"

"Will you stop and go away out and cut some hair!" Julia laughed.

"I will, and when I get back, we will sing it together. To celebrate Julia love, to celebrate!"

"Do you need me to go through it again, Nora?"

"We have been through it enough already," Nora snapped agitatedly.

"It needs to be right love. There will be skirmishes when the British are stung, raids, the police, army... People will need to stay strong."

"I'm afraid," she answered softly.

"Don't be," her husband reassured, taking her in his arms once more in.

Nora sighed and eased herself from his arms to stand.

"You were with me all day. I know what I have to do." There was a resignation in her voice that Donal chose to ignore.

"Good. It will be worth it."

"Will it?"

Donal kissed her. "It's going to be fine. So don't be worrying. This time tomorrow they will be cheering us in the streets, heroes. I'm sure of it."

Nora sat at the table in silence. She knew his mind was made up, and she struggled to suppress a tear.

"If it's what you want," she said, her voice barely audible.

"It is."

"And I can't say anything to make you change your mind?" Nora's words hung in the air.

"I must hurry," Donal replied quietly.

"Can't you stay a while longer?" she asked weakly.

"...I was thinking if it was a boy, Nora, we should call him after your father."

"Please, I could fix us up two nice mugs of tea, talk it through one more time."

"He would be proud of you this week Nora, his only daughter making a contribution. We will have all night to drink tea Nora, I promise."

And he was gone.

*

"Be Careful."

Bishop's Street.

Aungier Street.

Dame Street.

Harry lifted his head to soak in the familiarity of it all, the sun glistening off the cobblestones as he free-wheeled the final fifty yards. When the mood took him, he liked to dismount in motion and allow the bike to glide to a halt. It was a skill he had learned as a young child growing up on these very streets, and then to his left something incongruous also glistening in the spring sun and a figure crouched behind it.

Crack...

*

The shot echoed down Cork Hill and then a silence. Two crows whooshed into the city air as the cyclist crumpled. Donal felt frozen in the moment,

Doing what he was born for.

And then another sound broke the silence: *click, click, click* as the pedals wound to a halt.

Donal stood up slowly and gulped in the spring air, the gun still pointing and glistening in his hand.

Nora.

He had betrayed the one person who truly believed in him. He took a step forward. From his vantage point he could see a pool of blood and matter form around the motionless cyclist.

Crack...

Donal slumped. He tried to return fire, but was no longer in control. He jerked his head towards Dublin Castle desperately trying to adjust his dimming sight.

Nora.

Crack...Crack...

*

We will have all night to drink tea.

And he was gone.

And in his absence, thoughts of her own father, Seamus, consumed Nora.

He would be proud of you.

Maybe he would be she thought and when the police did call, she would indeed be brave, do her duty and *make her contribution.*

He was with me all day.

As she sat, she played it out over and over in her head and with each passing hour, she found herself slowly accepting that Donal had gone to do what he felt *born for*, that he was making a difference and that when he came through the door the next time, she would recon-cile all of that with him.

The little one kicked.

Seamus, if it's a boy.

*

Across town, Julia held Helen in her arms. "It won't be long now," she whispered. "Daddy will be home soon." She allowed herself a smile.

There was a song to be finished.

And On The Third Day

Monday

The early morning dew folded over the river like cling-film, and Seanie Dennehy took a moment to breathe it all in. He loved this time of the day before the city cranked into life. He scanned down the river to Parliament Bridge. The heron was there again.

Big Andy.

Seanie had recently taken to naming the various birds, wildlife, stray cats and dogs that traversed the quays. It was a familiarity that was a source of comfort to him, and occasionally, he found himself speaking quietly to them by name. At first, this habit which had crept up on him was unnerving, but he had his made peace with it.

Couldn't you be talking to worse?

"And what are you looking at this morning, Andy boy?"

The heron was also surveying the scene, Holy Trinity at its back, the heron a lone centurion. Soon it would be time to move on as the traffic and commuters began to snare along George's Quay, and Seanie always held its distinctive silhouette in his view as it glided into the distance.

Flying against the river again today...not good.

Seanie turned to his upturned punt. There was two hours solid work to be done. He needed to crack on and make a start while it was still quiet. He knew he wouldn't have the river to himself for long. Not today.

There would be family, friends and general do-gooders, but none of them would have a clue, of that you could be sure. There would be no talking to them.

Seanie set his toolbox down beside the punt and began to unpack an array of tools and battered paint tins. Finally, he unfolded an old *Evening Echo*, and kneeling on it gingerly he took a paint scraper in his hand. Soon he was lost in his thoughts, man and boat as one, as he worked at the bow of the upturned punt. The sounds of the city meant nothing to him now and then the youth, at first unnoticed...

Standing silently, scanning the river as intently as *Big Andy* had only moments earlier. Seanie placed the scraper down carefully and raised his head. Their gazes met.

"You're wasting your time there, boy, and the others too, all of ye. There won't be sign of him for three days. He'll be dragged down as far as here alright, but there's many a poor soul got brought into the mouth of the harbour by a current and were never found again. There's been loads of them," Seanie said, his voice measured, but the youth remained impassive.

"If I had a penny for every one of them," he continued.

"Oh, they'll dredge the river and put on a bit of a show for the family, but 'tis all bluff. No, if they don't pop up between here and the Northgate Bridge in three days you can throw your hat at it. You're in for the long haul, then."

"What?" the youth finally answered, his voice falling away.

"You're wasting your time," Seanie repeated.

"And what do you want us to do? Sit around at home, is it?" the youth shot back.

"I'm only telling you what I know boy, trying to make it easier for ye."

"Well, you're not, alright."

"Suit yourself," Seanie replied evenly, before taking the scraper back into his hand, adjusting his posture slightly and recommencing his work. Silence was their friend once more.

"I'm just saying it's too soon, that's all," Seanie's words hung in the air resignedly.

"For fuck's sake! You don't give up, do you!" the youth returned angrily.

"I've seen trained men gawk their hearts up, having to pull one out after three days. You haven't a fucking clue. Three days in there floating around," Seanie waved the scraper in the air like a conductor's baton. "Do you know what that does to a body. I can tell you straight, it's not a pretty sight."

The youth stepped through the railing from his vantage point on the footpath and onto the small wooden jetty. He was standing over the older man.

"Don't you worry about me at all. We're staying put until we get *Hayza* back, ok? Every one of us."

Both men fell silent, and the youth stepped forward on the timber platform closer to the river's edge.

What was it with young fellas and water? They come out of the pub steamed to the gills, and it's straight to the river they head.

"Thirty years I've been pulling them out along this stretch, thirty years. If I had a penny...," Seanie's voice trailed off and for the first time that morning he was aware of traffic noises as they bounced about the quay.

"Everything is a fucking penny with you. Have you ever heard of the euro!" the youth answered, raising his voice and wheeling aggressively from his standing point, but Seanie continued unflinchingly.

"There was a time when you would be pulling five or six a week and every one of them young fellas. Pub, pints and river."

"It wasn't like that," the youth replied, his voice a bare whisper. "I was there alright...he fell...slipped. We were talking."

"Talking? By the river?"

"Yes."

"Stone cold sober?"

"Would you get away from around me? Can't you see I'm busy!" the youth answered with a dismissive anger.

"You might as well be looking up the camel's ass, boy!"

Now the youth advanced on Seanie aggressively. "Who are you giving cheek to?" he demanded, stopping short at the older man.

"I know the *Lee* boy, every fucking ripple. You…you don't even know what you're looking out for. You're like all the young crowd going now. You can't tell them anything coz they think they know it all. Well, here's one for you…Ye don't!"

*

The old fiend was a complete head wreck.

Shane pulled his jacket tightly around himself.

What was keeping Lisa?

Hunger was taking hold and time had stood still. George's Quay had emptied out bar the occasional car and half-empty bus breaking the silence of the night air.

You're wasting your time.

Shane glanced at the punt once more, the work tidied up for the night.

"You might as well be looking up the camel's ass, boy," was his parting shot as he packed away his tools meticulously, neatly folded the stained *Evening Echo* and closed his toolbox at the end of another day. Shane had watched him closely as he manoeuvred his way through the railings and back onto the footpath. Crossing the street, he seemed frailer, less assured than he had been riverside, and then he was gone, merging seamlessly with the five o'clock, going home from work crowd.

Is that what he wants me to tell the family-this fiend with the boat-the camel's ass?

His words had cut deeply.

And they out last night doing everything they could, no sleep or food.

What the fuck was keeping her?

Shane flinched with the cold and finally, there she was.

At last.

The hood of her pink puffer jacket fighting a losing battle against the night chill, pink tracksuit bottoms *Juicy* and spattered *Uggs* that had seen better days. Lisa held the takeaway bag tightly to her tidy, expectant bump. A source of heat. A source of comfort.

"Sound Lisa girl! I'm bursting for a decent mangle," Shane exclaimed, his voice buoyant.

"You left me short two euro," she answered evenly as she handed over the food. Shane emitted a dismissive laugh, opening the bag eagerly.

"I'll have it for you tomorrow."

"You're some hump. Do you know that?" she reprimanded, but Shane was gorging himself on the hot food now, oblivious.

"It's only a scabby two euro. Did you get any drink?"

"Do you think I'm made of money?" she answered incredulously.

"Fuck it, Lisa. You have to have a drink, to wash it down like," he continued, eating rapidly. His complete focus was on the food, as if it needed to be consumed before some mysterious force might come and somehow magically vanish it all up before he could finish.

Lisa sat down delicately beside him, but all the while his head remained bowed, as if in adoration to the food.

"I'll be gasping now," he sputtered.

Pssh

Lisa had skillfully taken a can out of her pocket and opened it, unknown to him.

"Nice one Lisa girl!!"

"Who said anything about you?" she said mockingly.

Shane sat bolt upright and made a grab for the drink. "Just give us a shot off the can, will ya!"

"Get away!!" she laughed playfully, managing to hold the drink aloft out of Shane's reach.

"Come on. Don't be scanty," he pleaded, his right arm waving unsuccessfully in the air.

"That's another one sixty you owe me," she added finally, before handing him the drink.

"Yeah sound," he smiled before gulping the drink down.

"Pig," she said flatly, but Shane was wolfing and drinking in equal measure now.

The pair fell silent.

"Tis all on *Cork Beo* about *Hayza*," she said eventually.

"Most of it." His voice was cool.

"And it was a picture from my debs they used."

"I saw that, alright."

"And did you see the state of me in it, pure skinny, no fat or nothing," Lisa added animatedly.

"That's the baby shur."

"And *Hayza* is only handsome in it. They wanted to take another one today of me and his mam up at the

27

house. There was no way I was letting them do that." There was a tremor in her voice.

Shane folded out the takeaway wrapping across both their laps. "There's a few chips left there if you want 'em."

"You're some hound," she smiled, looking at the *brus* speckled across the grey paper.

"Do you want 'em or not?" he insisted.

"Jesus no! I'm big enough as it is already."

"I'll have 'em myself so," he said matter-of-factly.

Shane finished the crumbled remnants in silence, crumpled up the wrapping papers with a ceremonial fervour and tossed the grey mass at the punt. Both watched as it bounced off the wooden frame, rolled to the edge of the jetty stopping short of the water.

"You're alright now, are you?" Lisa said softly.

"Grand," he replied before emitting a loud belch. "That's the job!"

"Jesus!" Lisa recoiled from Shane's side.

"Ready for action now," he continued energetically, adjusting himself.

"*Hayza's* mam would crack altogether if she thought you were down here," Lisa said almost to herself.

"That's her problem, isn't it." His voice was cutting.

"There's no point in biting my head off over it. She just doesn't want you down here, that's all," she repeated.

"What was she saying?" Shane asked.

"That it was your fault in the first place." Her face flushed briefly.

"And how's that?"

"What happened like."

"I had nothing to do with it. We were just talking and he fell. Simple as."

"Well, she is blaming you," Lisa answered, trying to remain composed. She could sense Shane about to snap. She had seen that before, his eyes blinking rapidly.

"Fuck that!" Shane jumped to his feet. "I did everything I could to save him. It's not my fault at all. I'll tell her that too when I see her."

"Will you sit down," Lisa said calmly. "I wouldn't be going looking for her, that's all I'm saying."

Shane took her advice and sat reluctantly. "We were talking and he fell. He fucking fell, alright!"

"Just calm down, boy, will ya."

"Don't keep going on about it so," he replied.

"Ok," she said quietly. Lisa could hear Shane breathing hard.

"Just take it easy. And what were ye talking about?" she asked.

"I don't…I can't remember."

"And a load of *gatts,* I suppose."

"We were only after a few cans."

"And yokes?"

"Nothing, not a single yoke between us. God's honest truth." Shane threw his arms up in exasperation.

"He told me he was going asking for the money you owed him."

"He never mentioned anything to me, Lisa girl."

"So, it was just a few cans so," she continued, probing.

"Fuck it! How many times do I have to say it! Is that what you came down here for? To wreck my brain!" Shane could see that Lisa's eyes were starting to brim with tears.

"You are doing my head in over it," he mumbled.

Lisa began to sniffle awkwardly and Shane placed a consoling hand on her shoulder. "Look, I'm sorry. I'm just a bit freaked. 'Twas messy what happened him, and I was there. *Hayza* was A1, so he was."

"You're not the only one freaked. He was my fella," Lisa sniffled wiping her nose with the sleeve of her jacket.

"I thought it was all off between ye?"

Now it was Lisa's turn to exhibit anger. "Who told you that? That was nothing. Something stupid. What's it to you anyway?" she challenged.

"I'm only saying what I heard," he replied sheepishly.

"Well, you heard wrong."

Hayza

Shane had always thought *Hayza* was sound. Even after he blew him out.

"He didn't blow you out Shane," Lisa was adamant.

"That's what you say."

"'Twas you broke it off with me."

"Jesus Lisa."

"Don't start this again, Shane. Not here. Not now."

"I never said I was breaking it off," Shane tried to explain, but Lisa was tired of the futility.

"Fuck it Shane," she said curtly, cutting him off. "Now who is doing whose head in? Haven't I enough to be thinking about without you starting all this again!"

"I can't help it."

"Well try. I have a baby due in five months, you know."

"Is that all it is, five months."

"Yeah, that's all it is. Would you like to see my scan?" Lisa asked, taking the photograph from her pocket and holding it theatrically for Shane to take. He acquiesced, taking the image hesitantly and holding it from his body as if it was the actual newborn itself. He studied it briefly, perplexed. It reminded him of one of those, lunar surface of the moon shots, his Geography teacher Ms. Cronin bombarded them with from her overhead projector, all greys and blacks with a crater sitting centrally. There in the middle of the crater, sat for all the world, a slice of lemon.

He never like Miss Cronin.

"Will you relax," Lisa said assuredly. "Do you know anything. This way," she guided as she adjusted the scan in Shane's hand. Shane did as he was instructed and Lisa ran her index finger lovingly across the surface. "That's the head there," she pointed.

"It's a girl."

The slice of lemon.

"A girl," Shane whispered in awe.

"Chloe. I wanted Chloe for a girl."

"Chloe," he repeated inaudibly.

They shared the moment before Lisa cased the scan from his hand and went to return it to the safety of her pocket.

"Show it again there, will ya."

Lisa handed the scan back to Shane, and this time he studied it more knowledgably. "And it's definite, is it?"

"What?" she answered blankly.

"About the baby."

"What about it?"

"Do you know for sure like?"

"Amn't I just after saying it. Do you be listening to me at all boy?"

"That's not what I'm on about Lisa girl, and you know well it isn't," his voice cracked with desperation.

"Here, give me that," she answered. "You have it all pawed and everything. Jesus! And *Hayza* hasn't even seen it yet," Lisa said before wiping the image clean thrusting it into the recess of her pocket. Lisa's eyes looked tired now and her face weary, the countenance of a much older woman framed in a teenage body, and she stood up to leave.

"Look, I'm sorry, don't go," Shane said, indicating for her to sit back down.

"Just don't start again, alright."

"I won't. I promise," he agreed.

"Good," she managed, returning to sit.

"'Tis probably all a waste of time anyway," Shane continued.

"Is that what you think?"

"No, of course not. It's just someone was saying it," he replied, his eyes fixed firmly into the distance.

The camel's ass.

"Well off home with you so, if that's how you feel," Lisa shrugged.

"No I don't, honest," he tried to reassure her.

"When are you up?" she asked, trying to change the subject now.

"The fifteenth."

"And what's your probation officer saying?"

"I stopped going,"

"Jesus! You'll get done if you're not careful," her voice filled with genuine concern.

"They'll have to find me first. Fuck 'em."

"My social worker reckons I should go back and do the Leaving," Lisa said eventually.

"And who'll mind the child?"

"That's my business."

With that, Shane stared into the blackness of the river and thought better of probing Lisa more on her babysitting plans. He knew when not to rile her.

"Stay for a while though, Lisa, will you? Down here," he asked cautiously.

"The others will be looking for me."

"Just for a while to keep watch like."

"I don't know," Lisa mused.

"Go on, just for a while."

"Just for a while, so," she smiled weakly, resting her head on Shane's shoulder. She left it there momentarily, and he placed a comforting arm around her and pulled her close to offer some protection from the cold night air.

Tuesday

Seanie felt uneasy. He hadn't slept well.

The camel's ass.

Had he been too hard on the young lad? The lad meant well, but he was genuinely clueless. Them fellas in City Hall had fucked up the river good and proper. Digging up half the city for new buildings and putting most of them on marsh land. One decent shower of rain and the city flooded up to its eyeballs.

You can't treat the river like that.

No one in Europe treats their rivers like that. With every toss of his pillow, his own bitterness had stung him.

You're wasting your time.

There was a missing person, someone's child. He of all people should have known how that felt or maybe that was why he had said those words because he *did* know. Seanie slipped through the railings. The young lad was still there and now a girl, a bundle of pink sleeping soundly. Seanie crossed behind the punt choosing to ignore the pair. He picked up the bundled wrapping papers at the jetties edge.

"And you can be fined for that you know," he said disgustedly.

Shane shifted slightly. "Just fuck off old man. Go ahead and report me if you want."

"I've a good mind to. Christ we are a manky race," he attacked, stooping to pick up the drinks can also.

"Are you going to keep that up for the day?" Shane asked disparagingly.

"There's no law against it."

The voices brought Lisa to life, and she stretched slowly like a ballerina from a deep slumber. "What time is it ?" she asked, her joined hands pointing skywards.

"No time for a young one like you to be out and about in a place like this," Seanie reprimanded as he began to set up his workstation for the day. The stranger's voice quickly brought Lisa to her senses. She jumped to her feet and adjusted herself in one swift movement. "Jesus Shane! I'll be murdered! Why didn't you wake me? I'm supposed to be looking after myself."

"I didn't want to when you were sleeping like," Shane answered awkwardly.

"Jesus Shane, are you thick or what?"

"I thought you wanted to stay on. To look for *Hayza.*"

"It's at home you should be, girl. Getting your proper sleep," Seanie said directly. "Shur if anything happens on the river I'll be the first to know. I keep telling him that," he added, jerking a calloused thumb in Shane's direction.

"You do," Shane agreed contemptuously. "Every five minutes."

"I know the river, young one, every last inch of it," Seanie continued, choosing to ignore Shane's latest barb.

"Not this again," Shane countered.

"Shh Shane, will ya," Lisa said, gesturing at him to be quiet. "And who are you when you are out?" she demanded.

"I've told him it's all about the currents, but shur what would I know," Seanie's voice trailed off as he turned from the young couple and commenced his morning toolbox ritual.

"And can you find him?" Lisa asked, approaching slowly.

Seanie raised his head. "If he's there to be found."

"What do you mean by that?" Her voice was steady.

"Well there was a girl one time went into the water the night of her twenty-first in the boat club, nobody knows what happened to her. The night of her twenty-first imagine. Anyway, they dredged the river for days and there was a crowd like yourselves out all hours of the day and night and not a sign of her. I was in *Dunlops* at the time and the lads even gave over their lunch breaks looking for her, but nothing for weeks. You're only two days yet."

"Jesus," Lisa exhaled.

"And then one day this fella is out minding his own business with his auld dog and there she is washed up in front of him. I'm sure t'was the auld dog that spotted her first, but here's the thing…in fucking Wales no less, Wales, beat that in two throws if you can. There was nothing left of the poor child, nothing, a watch and a ring. Two presents, I'm sure." Seanie left his words hang in the morning air.

"Jesus, did you have to tell us that," Lisa exclaimed.

"And you're worse to be listening to him." Shane responded.

"She'd only stepped out for a bit of air. A simple thing."

"You're giving me the creeps now," Lisa said miserably.

"A watch and a ring," Seanie added thoughtfully.

At this Shane stood quickly to comfort Lisa. "Don't take any notice of him Lisa girl. He's talking shite since I got here."

"Have it your own way so," Seanie finished, and he began to unfold the *E*vening *Echo* neatly alongside the punt.

"I'll talk to him if I want to Shane, ok," Lisa chided, stepping away from Shane's advance.

"The fiend hasn't a clue what he is on about Lisa. That's what I'm trying to tell you." There was an urgency in Shane's voice now, but Lisa was ignoring Shane and all her attention was on the stooped older man. "Can you help us or not?" she asked firmly, leaning in closer to Seanie. He cleared his throat. "I know the places to look...places no one knows," he said confidently.

*

For Nora Hayes, sleep was the enemy ever since the news broke. Twice it had taken hold, and now she was prepared to fight it with every fiber of her being. The first time was when she lay on the bed after the neighbours had plied her with copious amounts of strong tea, *for the awful shock*. She had needed to find space, to take it all in. She had woken some time later, disorientated, and for one wondrous moment between sleep and waking, her only son Gary was not missing. Sitting up sharply, her heart sank unceremoniously.

The second time crept up on her unannounced as she sat by the fire. Then the sleep came in waves, and she dreamed vividly of meeting Ronnie Drew, dressed in a hi-vis river rescue jacket, on point-duty at the door of her local *The Cotton Ball*. He looked well, younger than she imagined, and he had advised her sagely not to go in. Inside, family and friends were crowded around a small TV screen celebrating wildly. She struggled to get a clear vantage point, and she appeared invisible to the cheering throng. Finally, she broke through and on the flickering screen she could see him with a beaming smile, Shane Buckley, holding a trophy aloft and declaring jubilantly above the din. "*Hayza* is back in his rightful home!" She woke with a start.

Shane Buckley.

The dream began to fade like a sea mist. She struggled to retain it, to make sense.

Shane Buckley.

That much remained clear.

He had some nerve showing his face on the riverbank. Brass neck.

He had told her he had done everything to save him.

Gary, her only son. Ran away, that's what he did.

To get help, he called it.

Left my Gary like that in the water. It's a fucking hiding he should get. Her poor Gary. And Michael, that tool of a father of his on the riverbank wearing that hi-vis jacket.

She had barely recognised him when he turned up.

Ronnie Drew.

"He's my son too, you know," Michael had said lamely.

"It never bothered you before."

"Christ, Nora, let it go."

It was like old times.

When Gary was born, there had been a period of respite, both herself and Michael, Gary's father, keeping up appearances, but this suspension of hostilities was brief. Nora threw herself into raising Gary and bounced Michael out the door like a punctured football.

Let it go. Is that all he could say? After all this time.

And later-riverside

"'Twas an accident, Nora."

"So they keep telling me," she answered without an ounce of respect.

"No one's fault."

"Everything is someone's fault if you go back far enough."

"You don't mean that," Michael had answered, his voice low.

"Don't I?"

"You wouldn't have said it one time."

"That's what rearing a child on your own does for you," she hissed in reply.

"Twas you threw me out," Michael snarled.

"And with good reason. Are you still with that young one?" Nora asked casually.

"Catherine?"

"Yeah, that one from Douglas."

"She's not from Douglas."

"She's still on the scene so." Nora's voice was pinched.

"She is," he answered coldly.

"And who's minding her to-night? Her mammy and her daddy?" Nora continued caustically.

"Christ, Nora, you never give up, do you?" His voice was strained.

Nora took a step back and looked at Michael straight in the face. The hi-vis jacket was ill-fitting, a beacon of yellow against the dull surrounds of the riverbank, *Cork River Rescue Volunteer*, emblazoned both front and back. He looked incongruous to her, like an adman who had strayed off his pitch.

"What are doing here, Michael? Can you explain that to me?" she asked earnestly. The question seemed to catch Michael off-guard. "What do you think I'm-I'm doing here?" he stammered.

"I don't know, showing your face." Nora threw her arms up quizzically.

"Jesus, you're some cold bitch when you want to be."

"That's more like it, the Michael I know and love so well," she laughed.

"Fuck it, Nora."

"And is young Catherine ever a cold bitch when she wants to be?"

"Stop it," he pleaded.

"Or don't they have that class of thing in Douglas."

"Stop it, I said!!" Michael roared through clenched teeth, raising a fist in anger.

Nora turned away. "The old Michael," she said flip-pantly.

"Are you fucking happy now? Are you?" Michael's voice was filled with emotion.

"Are you?" Nora continued, persistently.

"She loves me, so I am Nora, yes. You remember what that feels like?"

Nora stood defiantly, her back to the lapping water. "Love, don't make me sick," she taunted.

"Just button it, Nora, will you," he answered angrily.

"Or what?"

Michael fell silent.

"You'll hit me a few belts, is it? Don't talk to me about love boy," she said with a pitiful voice.

"She's pregnant, ok," Michael blurted out.

"What?" Nora suppressed a laugh.

"Yes, with my child. That's how much she loves me."

"So that's why you came, is it? To rub my nose in it."

"I came because I wanted to come. This is my loss too," Michael said in a cracked whisper. "I wanted to do the decent thing," he continued.

"Knocking up young ones. Is that what they are calling decency now?" Nora barked with a renewed anger, and she turned from Michael to face the river. He stood defeated.

"Christ, Nora, how did we ever let things get this bad," he said finally, a sadness consuming his eyes. "Do you really hate the sight of me that much?"

Nora turned to face him once more, and she spoke without feeling. "I've had good practice."

"I said I was sorry a long time ago for all of that," he shrugged.

"You did."

"And I meant it."

"And that's supposed to make everything alright," Nora finished, her voice welling up.

"No, of course not, but I was *ga-ga* from the drink back then. I didn't want to hurt you at all."

Nora was no longer looking at him but staring into the distance. Finally, she spoke.

"And what's your excuse this time?"

"A fresh start, Nora."

"With a one half your age." Her voice sounded disillusioned. Michael did not reply.

"You want to do the decent thing. Stay away from here, Michael. You're not welcome."

Wednesday

Shane didn't know what to feel, vindicated that their trip *had* all been a waste of time and had shown the old man up for what Shane believed him to be all along, or gutted that as the old man edged the punt alongside the jetty that he had not delivered what he had promised.

I know the places to look.

Shane was cold, wet and miserable. They all were. It was well past midnight. The old man had barely muttered on the return trip up river, all confidence evaporated, and now in the gloom of the jetty he looked gaunt. Shane had given his jacket to Lisa in a vain effort to keep her warm on the journey. The old man had called that right.

It was at home she should be.

Shane knew that now. He allowed his mind to wander, the neon hue from The Elysian Tower drawing him in comfortingly. He thought for a moment what it might be like to live in that glass bubble high above the city, to sit by day and watch the ants scurrying about their business or by night to perch as the city revealed its darkest secrets. To watch and to see. The three of them.

Looking up the camel's ass.

"I told you it wasn't a trip for young ones." Seanie Dennehy's voice was stern.

Nobody answered.

"The next few hours will tell a tale."

Shane helped Lisa navigate the last steps onto the jetty. He glanced back down into the punt. Seanie Dennehy was securing the ropes. He seemed to be talking to no one in particular as the punt swayed gently.

"Aye, they certainly will."

Shane had had enough. "Do you know what? I'm sick of your fucking bullshit and pissing about on the river for hours. What did that get us? Come on, Lisa, let's get out of this kip before he kills the lot of us."

Lisa stood transfixed. Frozen in motion.

"Come on Lisa. We don't have to listen to anymore of his shite."

"Just give him a hand up, will ya." Her voice seemed remote.

Shane shook his head in disbelief. "There, happy now," and he hauled the old man unceremoniously onto the jetty. Seanie Dennehy adjusted himself. "Listen, the both of ye. I've seen too many families waiting and families praying and then being reduced to a slice of luck. A fella walking his dog in Wales, for fuck's sake. I wouldn't wish that on anyone."

And he was gone.

*

Shane and Lisa stood disconsolately on the jetty. It was as if to move would bring the closure nobody wanted. They had watched silently as Seanie Dennehy faded into the distance.

I wouldn't wish that on anyone.

The water lapped gently. It would be daylight soon. To leave was to lose.

"And you were right all along, you know," Lisa said, her voice trailing off. "About *Hayza* and me."

"What about ye?" Shane answered, his voice clipped.

"We weren't together. Not for two weeks. And now this…"

"Don't take any notice of me," he replied dismissively.

"We weren't."

"Come here will ya," Shane said, approaching to comfort her. "Tis messy what's after happening, but it's not your fault, and anyway you can't be sure, not for certain, not without a test or something."

Lisa stopped abruptly.

"Christ Shane, for once and for all, it's not your child ok! I know who the father is." Her voice was raised.

"I'm only saying what *Hayza* said to me," he continued, his mouth tightening.

"What? What was he saying about it? Did you say something to him?" Lisa asked firmly, taking two steps back from Shane now, fixing her eyes on him squarely. In the half-light, he suddenly seemed frail and shrunken. Without warning, she stepped forward forcefully, their faces almost touching. "You did, didn't ya!" she demanded urgently.

"No." His voice was weak.

Lisa turned and walked away in disgust.

"Fuck it, Shane. You couldn't keep your big mouth shut!"

"Will you let me explain," Shane pleaded.

"So, you did say something!" she exclaimed, turning to face him once more. Her eyes were hard now and her face flushed. "Christ, I should have listened to his mam!" Lisa wheeled away and began climbing ferociously through the railings on to the footpath. There standing above him, she gripped the railings in anger.

"Some cheek you have boy and me defending you," she attacked, her voice choked with emotion.

"For fuck's sake Lisa will you listen," he begged once more, summoning all the energy he could muster from his tired, aching body.

"Twas he pushed me first!"

*

When the truth finally broke, it spilled across George's Quay in unrelenting waves, each new revelation buffeting Lisa where she stood. As it cascaded around her, she no longer gripped the railings in defiance but for support.

The truth.

How *Hayza* had spent the whole night mocking Shane about the baby, taunting him that he had, "a lucky escape," as he put it, calling Lisa "a tramp and stuff."

And of how Shane had kept telling him to stop, but he wouldn't. "What would you do about it?" he had goaded.

Before the final detail of Shane trying to explain to Lisa that she knew. "The way *Hayza* can get sometimes," as he outlined the gut-wrenching denouement of how *Hayza* had pushed him hard in the chest and, "I just went to lock on to him, and he just stumbled back like…He slipped. We were talking and he slipped. He fell."

George's Quay fell silent.

"Say something Lisa. You believe me, don't you. That he fell."

"Does it matter what I believe?"

"It does to me. I couldn't let him say all those things about you and the baby."

"So, you pushed him in the river over it."

*

Lisa's mind was made up. The last hour had been a complete blur, Shane banging on about wanting to be part of her life, the baby's life, how they could…

They.

Her plans were made. A proper start for Chloe with a good decent foster family and a second chance for Lisa to make a fresh start, get educated and do something with her life. Lisa knew it was the right thing to do, knew all along, knew before the scan, before *Hayza*... She had talked it through with her social worker.

A good foster family-for the baby's sake.

Nothing was standing in the way of that.

"And what about me and what I want," Shane had repeated over and over again, but Lisa remained steadfast.

Nothing.

"And I'm telling you, if you go making trouble for me Shane or the baby, I won't be long letting the *shades* know who pushed who in the river!"

"What?" he replied with a flash of anger.

"I fucking will," Lisa had replied through gritted teeth.

"I'll rat you out."

*

Nora Hayes had meant it when she told Michael he was not welcome. She had plenty of regrets in life, but not in that department.

Knocking up young ones.

And she had felt relieved when the little one had told her she was giving the child up.

She was only a child herself.

She had thought about that for Gary, but they were different times. You would have never dreamed of saying it.

You made your bed.

She couldn't. She felt too selfish in the end and he lost his chance. It had gnawed at her these last three days. Thoughts she had suppressed for twenty years.

What might have been-for everyone.

Today made her feel…

Her phone pinged.

*

Lisa looked at her phone fearfully.

"There's news," she said, her voice filled with dread.

"*Hayza,*" Shane breathed slowly, opening his own device robotically.

"They've found him, Lisa."

The young girl crumpled to her knees. From the jetty, Shane watched impassively. There was no comfort he could offer. Her words had cut him deep. They were finished.

Rat.

Thursday

The old fiend was right after all. Three days he said.

Three days.

Shane wanted to square that with him. Give credit where credit was due. He had passed the house on his way down to the city. The front door was open and a couple of neighbours were smoking, their voices hushed. He pulled up his hood. He knew where he was not wanted. At Mayfield Garda Station, he crossed the road quickly. He said what he had to say, given his statement, done his duty. If he didn't cause her any trouble, he should be ok. He comforted himself with that. Lisa would be good to her word. If what they had ever meant anything, she would do that for him at least.

He fell.

There was nothing to be gained by anything else. He moved quickly as the city sprawled before him.

Ants going about their business.

On the riverbank, someone had already tied a single rose at the spot. It flapped in its plastic. Shane stopped sharply to read the inscription.

Never forgotten bud
RIP
From all at Village FC

Shane allowed himself a smile. He couldn't remember the last time *Hayza* had kicked a ball. The sun had broken through and Shane stood in the silence.

Flap...flap...flap.

His upper body twitched. This wasn't how he remembered this place.

The city's secrets.

He moved on.

At George's Quay, Seanie Dennehy was setting up for the day.

"You got it all wrong, didn't you," Shane scoffed. "Admit it."

"And what do you mean by that?"

"Shur didn't they find him only fifty yards from where he went in and you blowing on about how you could be dragged down as far as here or even end up in Wales. Wales my hole."

"What did you say?". Seanie Dennehy stood bolt up-right.

"I'm just saying, you didn't do us much good, that's all."

"I've given this river a lifetime boy, twenty-four seven."

"So," Shane shrugged.

"So! To save people going through what I went... hours, days, weeks, months of it. And not a sign of her."

"Of who?"

"My own daughter boy, that's who."

*

Shane tried as best he could to get his head around it. A watch and a ring were all Seanie Dennehy had been left with. His only daughter.

Wales.

He didn't know what to say, like he hadn't known what to say to Lisa, only this was different, now he had wanted to say something, but the words wouldn't come. The old man took charge, made it easier for him.

"Ah, nobody cares, boy," he said with an ill at ease laugh.

"But how do you know that for sure like"

"I'm not going to see much more of you around here, am I?" he answered pointedly.

"No, I mean, I can't." Shane's voice was flustered. "My probation officer wants me to do a course or something, says it would look good with the judge, stop me getting done like."

Seanie Dennehy nodded in agreement.

"And what about you?" Shane asked.

"I'm a beaten bird by. I didn't do ye much good," Seanie answered wearily.

"I didn't mean that."

"Thanks boy. No, the writing is on the wall. Search and rescue is coming. There will be no place for an old codger like me in all of that, training courses, ten-thousand-pound boats. I'm past it, boy."

"But you called it right," Shane contradicted. "Three days, you said."

"I did."

"Three days."

*

Seanie Dennehy was alone again, the way he liked it. The young fella had meant well and had stayed beyond what was reasonable. Seanie had wished him well and "hoped it all worked out" for him. He wasn't a bad lad, and Seanie had watched him walk away up George's Quay and blend into the distance at Parliament Bridge. The heron was on the late shift today, impervious to the evening traffic.

Big Andy.

As Seanie watched, the bird rose majestically and began to make its way in tandem with the river's flow.

"Good," Seanie thought to himself contentedly. Seanie held the bird in his gaze as it passed overhead.

"A penny for your thoughts big Andy bud, a penny for 'em," he said aloud.

It was always pennies with Seanie.

Aisling

Clown *n,* **jester; fool, anarchist – clown'ish** *a* **, persecutor**
Mother (Muth-) n, female parent; act as a mother to – to give care and attention – motherly a, protector

  I'm your idea. I was last year and I am today. You wanted the clown in situ before they arrived, and I am back again. Said everything had to be just right, you called it back, the official blurb:
  Giggles, serving up belly-laughs since 2007, birthdays, christenings, weddings.
  My parties are a BLAST
  That's me!
  The party.
  And clowns see things, feel things, the dynamic, first impressions-like from the off, he was having none of it.
  The expense.
  Hired a professional.
  Ridiculous! Every snotty-nosed kid in the estate traipsing through the house. And for what?
  Guaranteed squeals of delight.

The children.

Kids.

Never envisaged myself as a mother. Didn't think I'd cope, and then you see other couples, your friends settling into the familiarity of it all. The natural feel of it and then in the blink of an eye, that's you too.

Took to it like a duck to water.

And when he first held the twins.

Brought him to his knees.

Especially Jan.

A proper Daddy's girl.

But the novelty wears off. The being there. The Breakfasts, lunches, school runs, basketball, gymnastics.

The fucking price of it! To jump around. Could they not do that in the fucking park for free!

Turned a blind eye to that.

Thought he'd change.

Hoped.

Did we ever love him? Take time, but an answer is definitely needed. Come now. At any stage did you ever…was there ever any love between Aisling and the man she took in matrimony for better or worse? No fudging. Address the issue at hand. It's beneficial. Come now. A simple yes or no will suffice.

Do we ever really know someone, I mean really know them?

That's not the question.

The confusion.

That's a no, from me!

No.

Never even considered the seriousness of your marriage vows.

No, I never…

Making Aisling responsible for the course of events.

Not true! It wasn't like that.

Answer the question.

Stop! I could have.

Could have, would have, should have.

No one understands.

Guilty as charged.

My every word twisted.

Pull yourself together, woman! We'll have a smoke. That's what we'll do.

Smoking. That drove him daft altogether.

The last bastion of pleasure. Drop the kids to school, home, house to yourself.

Cup of coffee.

Fag.

A few sneaky biscuits.

The feet up.

And a straight face when he came home later.

You were smoking again. Kids, did you see Mammy smoking those ugly dirty things today?

Getting my own children to spy on me.

And later.

You would want to try and do something about that little belly you are putting on. Could you not walk them to school?

The hurt.

Make me laugh.

It's no laughing matter.
The party...all of this...was...is my idea.
Laughter, today?
You're here on my say so.
Hired a professional.
Thought long and hard about it.
A sensible decision.
Make me laugh so. Something funny. You come and go as I please.
Thoughts make fools of us.
That's what attracted me to him.
A wise guy. I like that in a man.
At the start, always had some joke or other.
They dry up fast.
He had a good head for them though, and the ones he'd tell over and over again, like the one about the magician.
On the Titanic.
Working away grand until this guy comes in with a parrot on his shoulder.
So, the magician makes a rabbit disappear.
And the parrot goes, "It's under the table." Then the magician makes a dove disappear and the parrot goes again, "The table, the table."
Which really pissed off the magician.
So anyway, let me see, oh yeah, the ship hits the iceberg and the whole thing goes down, but the magician, he's like Leonardo DiCaprio, and he manages to swim his way to the top and grab hold of a piece of timber. And you'd never guess who is on the other end of it?
Let me see now. Let me see now.

Yep, our friend the parrot and they just stared at each other and said nothing. The magician eyeing the parrot and the parrot eyeing the magician.

And this went on for one day, two days and a third day.

And finally, the parrot looks the magician straight in the face and says…I give up. Where's the fucking ship!

Bravo!

They should have been here by now.

And the clown in situ.

Sorry, I don't know what came over me.

Feel free to share.

Sometimes the melancholy gets…

Gets you down.

Yes.

Understandable.

And you try and hold your end up as best you can.

Him, the twins, the house.

Exactly, but lately, it's like this dream I've been having.

Over and over again.

Me filling this sandpit with water, back and forth, bucket after bucket, until the dream ends and…

The trench is dry.

Jesus!

You're tired.

What do you know?

Since last year.

Last year was different.

We were waiting then too. You and the clown.

I didn't want to live here in the first place.

He wanted that.

And his parents. Had notions that way. Thought I wasn't good enough for their white-haired boy.

Aisling never got above her station. Go on, get it all off your chest.

We got married after a year.

A whirlwind romance.

He had a fear of being an old father, never said it, but with the age gap and all.

Gold digger!

I think his parents thought the marriage was a panic measure on his part, but I never felt like that. If only he wasn't always so worried about what others thought. He was so...

Insecure.

I didn't go in totally blind. I knew all about before, how everything had been planned right down to the wedding band and how she had pulled the plug last minute and took him for ten thousand at the credit union.

He did get the ring.

And me on the rebound.

Are we starting to believe that now?

I just wish I didn't feel so cut off.

Reporting for duty!

Fun and games. If only.

Guaranteed squeals of delight.

Do you know what I would like?

Haven't a scoobies.

To slip away. When our problems started, they rained down in twos and threes, body blows until we just couldn't make the money last. Evenings without two words between us. I tried to make it work. I bloody tried. The priest told us to "have another child" to "steady things." For fuck's sake.

Cut this self-indulgent crap. What did our parents do? People are always whining nowadays. Can we not just roll up our socks and get on with it, instead of the same fucking questions, round and round and round? The foot should have been put down day one, living beyond one's means and nothing on the table, only banana fucking sandwiches. Jesus wept!

He began to drift.

Are we going through all this again?

And again, if needs be.

It serves no purpose.

It serves every purpose because before my eyes the man I thought I knew, the man I married, he changed and not he nor I...

Could do a thing about it. Big deal. Now where the fuck are they?

All it had to be was a straightforward party. Was that too much to ask?

They're not coming.

The clown knew first.

Sees things. And then the penny dropped, calmly at first and then screaming it around the estate.

Squealing.

As if it was the clown's fault.

The clown knew.

A full hour had passed. You rang his work, remember.

Told me he had left early to pick up the kids from school.

That wasn't the plan. He never picked the kids up from school.

The penny dropped.

Never.

What makes a man do that?

Well, there are a number of aspects which we'd need to clarify. If we could do that at this stage, it would make things easier later on. Take your time, but was there anything to suggest that maybe your husband wasn't himself, any small domestic issue, perhaps you took no notice of. I know it's difficult, but anything at all would help. Was everything, ok, between ye?

The suggestion that it was fault. That I drove him to it.

That's the guards for you.

And the answer to my question?

What makes a man go and do what he did?

As if I had something to do with it. Went through all that with the counsellors, how it became so that he hated himself and had to take his revenge out on everyone else.

The man wasn't right upstairs.

But to do what he did.

To the ones he loved.

He never collected the kids.

And you never saw it coming.

Should I have?

Caught up in the party, everything being just so. Hired a professional. Guaranteed squeals of delight.

Squeals.

Never suspecting.

That this was the day he had chosen to collect the kids and travel down through the quays to a spot on the river where they'd never been before. Oh, Jesus!! Why the children? Even if it had been just himself, but my babies too…

They say that's how such minds work.

Waiting, but they were never coming.

And today?

The clown is back on my terms.

It was going to be such a great day, every snotty-nosed kid in the estate. No expense spared.

Hired a professional.

Where did that year go?

He had his own plans.

Where does that leave us?

Broken.

You said it. That's the hard part.

You live an honest decent life and one day the roof caves in, and you've no control anymore, and it's a horrible, horrible feeling.

For a horrible, horrible year.

And I'm not facing another one.

Is that your…final answer?

Final.

Snap.

Before the Houses

Everybody agreed that Dolly Sheehan could hold a tune:

Whatever happened to the famous five?
Now we're happy just to be alive.
Whatever happened to the dreams we held?
Now we question all that we said.
The famous five...

And now, 1979 still remained vivid, crystal clear, especially the sounds of that summer. Katie listened attentively as her mother's voice trailed off, and she adjusted the wheelchair in front of the bay window. Katie hummed the tune to a close softly. "There now mam, that's lovely."

Dolly scanned the familiar vista in silence. Once all you could see from that spot were big deciduous trees, trees as far as the eye could see, and when she had arrived first Katie used to take her down amongst them. It had been recommended by the staff as part of the *settling-in* process. Dolly used to like that, **the kind one**, how she'd take her down and let her pick-

But not today.

"They'll be putting roofs on the last of those houses soon," Dolly whispered to herself solemnly.

"They will mam."

"Hey!" Dolly continued, raising her voice. "Hey…put me to bed," she continued, waving a wizened hand at the window.

"Hey! Put me to bed, bitch!"

"Mam," Katie reprimanded, tiredly, but her mother continued to wave.

"All bitches, the lot of them."

"It's ok mam." Katie's voice was soothing.

"Shh, say nothing," Dolly offered conspiratorially, raising her head. **The young one was kind, not like the others. The young one brought the sweets.**

"Say nothing girl. Do you see him in the garden?" Dolly asked, pointing ET-like into space.

"I do mam."

"If that fella gets wind of the sweets, he'll eat me out of house and home." **No, the young one would not let that happen. She was kind. Kind like Katie.**

*

79 was that glorious summer in Courtown. The three of them, herself, Tom – **that man** and Katie. That's when Dolly had spotted it first, the kindness. They had made friends with that family from Kilkenny, the Kelly's and their little one Julia, a little slip of a thing, not a pick of her there.

She could still remember that and of how Katie had begun hiding her food and then following her one evening and there they were down by a rock pool with Katie sharing, her beautiful Katie, sharing her sandwiches with the little Kelly girl. Taking them from a tissue. **The kind one.**

79 Courtown, and then…**he died, that man.**

Asking them all to pray for him on his deathbed.

Hail Mary, full of grace. The Lord is with thee.

And Katie weeping that night in the Infirmary, uncontrollably, when **that man** had asked that and more. The priest saying privately that it was too big an ask, even from a father, for a young girl that age with her whole life in front of her, that it wasn't right, natural even, to make someone so young promise, amidst all that grief, to look out for her mother.

And Katie keeping that promise, caring for her mother, looking after her on the days she could not get out of her bed, holding Dolly's hand and helping to wish away the grief.

The kind one.

"For fuck's sake, someone put me to fucking bed!"

"Mam, please!"

*

Katie was there the first night her mother forgot, her words.

Hail Mary full of…

"A slip of the tongue", Dolly had reasoned, but Katie wouldn't let it go, keeping her promise to her father and insisting her mother get it seen to. "Just in case it's something more sinister." And then becoming the reassuring voice that they could get through this together, just before it all went wrong.

"I just got confused, that's all. Is that a crime? They all look the same, streets, houses, streets, houses, so many houses. I wasn't fucking lost!"

*

"Please, mam, just don't…shout."

"The kind one puts me to bed and used to take me down by the trees, in the beginning, for a chat and she'd hold my hand. I liked that."

"I liked it too, mam."

"And then we'd pick…just the two of us. Before the houses. Before your man there. Do you see him?"

"I do mam," Katie nodded, her voice choked with emotion.

"Would you ever go away and have a shave for yourself, boy," Dolly commanded. "There's no sweets for you today, no sweets," she laughed mockingly. "Go on, tell him there's no sweets, no sweets."

"I will mam."

*

Katie had agonised over the final decision -*we can get through this together*- but in the end she couldn't cope, telling her mother that this place, St. Ottern's Nursing Home, was indeed the best place for the both of them.

66

She had stood her ground tearfully when Dolly had pleaded for "one more chance," admonishing Katie for breaking her promise to **that man**, of never leaving her alone. The accusation hurt, but Katie was determined.

"We both suffered enough mam."

She encouraged her mother to "give it time," and listened intently over the months to Dolly's worries about time, about "the trees going one by one, day by day, before the houses."

The sweets smoothed over everything.

*

"Did you bring the sweets, the jellies, the ones I like?"

"I did mam."

"Quick give them there to me before your man gets wind of them. Do you see him in the garden, that fella with the beard?"

"I do mam," Katie answered, taking her mother's hand in hers.

"You're the kind one," Dolly said glumly.

"Mam, it's me, Katie, your Katie."

"Bitch."

Katie hugged her mother, fighting back the tears.

"I will say…"

"What mam, what do you want to say?"

"I don't feel on top of the world."

"I'm here mam, it will be fine," Katie answered, squeezing her mother's hand softly.

"And I don't know where I am."

"I know where you are, and I love you," Katie whispered and wiped away a tear.

"You're a nice girl."

Katie hugged her mother once more, this time holding her upper body close to hers.

"My mind is all mixed up." Her mothers bare whisper now agitated.

"I promised to look after you, after dad, do you remember that mam?" Katie hinted kindly.

"And you do."

"And we've had some wonderful memories," Katie continued, clearing her throat.

"Before the houses"

"And I'll remember those days mam, for the both of us."

"Put me to bed, love, will you? I just want the pillow."

"I will, and the next time I will bring some Foxgloves for your locker. You'd like that, wouldn't you?"

"The nice girl used to let me pick those."

"We did."

"Down by the trees, before the…"

Katie released the brake from the wheelchair and eased gently away from the window.

"Come on so, and we will get you all snug."

"You're a nice girl, a kind girl, just like our own little one. Have I told you that before?" Dolly asked, staring ahead.

"You have mam."

Katie eased the wheelchair across the wooden floor.

"Do remember Courtown mam?" she asked cautiously before she began to sing softly.

We held our future in our hands,
Though we did not know it then,
Sitting on a park bench,
Thinking it would never end.

Katie allowed her voice to trail off, but continued to hum that sound of 79 as they made steady progress down the long hallway to the bedrooms. Slowly, her mother picked up the tune of her daughter's soft lilt, and she began to sing sweetly.

Whatever happened to the famous five?
Now we are happy just to be alive.

Dolly Sheehan, still holding a tune like she always did.

Our Man in Baghdad

Bryan O'Byrne *always* felt the urge to go just before he went live. He blamed the adrenaline. Ten years of experience of reporting from war zones all over the world and that was the one constant, *simply bursting for a sluice*. It was a foible that the many floor managers and directors he worked with knew well, and they always tried to make allowances for it when counting him in. As he stood on the roof of The Palestine Hotel Baghdad ready to file his report, Caroline Casey, back in the comfort of her Irish TV studio, knew it also. But the Bryan she knew was nothing if not a perfectionist and in many years of segues had never found himself caught short on live TV and had never embarrassed any colleagues. Caroline took a deep breath and went where the teleprompter took her…

As U.S. troops consolidate their hold on Baghdad International Airport, the Iraqi president has been quoted as saying that Baghdad will be defended against international invaders. Following what local residents have described as a night of hell we can now go to our man in Baghdad, Bryan O'Byrne, from where he sends this report.

And there he was. Pink sleeveless shirt, helmet, flak jacket, perma-tan, empty bladder and ready to rock and roll. The ultimate professional...

Yes, it certainly was the night from hell as you mentioned there Caroline with Saddam Hussein International Airport coming under sustained attack from U.S. led forces and bombing raids continuing throughout the night and lighting up the sky around us. In fact, one source tells us that the American F18 fighters have met little resistance and that there is up to one thousand U.S. troops active in and around the airport, but this has been difficult to confirm.

And he was gone, Caroline wishing him well advising him to take care.

And in other news...

Dick—she thought to herself.

*

"You're a complete dick, Bryan, you know that don't you," Caroline said, her voice filled with annoyance. "A self-absorbed dick." She sat on the end of the bed, her back glistening from where she had been unable to dry. He found the droplets erotic.

"I just want to talk," he answered sitting forward his hand on her lower back where she sat.

"Now, this minute." Caroline stood, allowed the towel slip to the floor, stepped from it and walked to her overnight bag. There she dutifully selected a lace thong. He watched her step gracefully into it, pull it up delicately and adjust it around her taut behind. Bryan had enjoyed this last six months. The excitement of it all, their weekly trysts at various hotel locations across Dublin and occasionally, when the opportunity had arisen, she letting him stay over at her Ballsbridge apartment. He wanted more. Caroline stepped into the bathroom, where she began applying makeup artfully from an array of brushes.

"What about?" she called out offhandedly.

"Us."

"And can it not wait, this talk? I mean to-night of all nights."

Caroline stepped back in to the bedroom and took a sequined ball gown from the wardrobe.

"Is there ever a good time?" he answered, leaning back against the headboard.

Caroline carefully removed the dress from its hanger, placed it over her head, and shimmied her body into the outfit.

"I haven't time for this now," she said firmly as she made some final adjustments in front of the mirror. She turned to face him.

"How do I look?"

"Jesus, phew," he emitted a long breath.

She waited for more.

"It's not too…see-through, is it?" Her voice seeking reassurance.

"You know right well it is," he laughed.

Caroline turned to examine herself in the mirror once more. She liked how the material accentuated her shape. Her breasts looked firm, her nipples pert.

Jewelled.

This would certainly turn heads on to-night's red carpet, curry favour with a few execs.

"It's not too much," she continued doubtfully.

"A-mazing!" Bryan's gaze delved deep.

Caroline was pleased. She was the main news anchor, and presenting these awards was a new departure for her career and would open some new doors. She needed to be eye-catching but also discreet, to get the balance right. She looked at herself once more in the mirror.

Sexy but subtle.

"Zip me up so," she quipped, a sense of satisfaction in her voice.

Bryan stepped from the bed, crossed the room and did as instructed as they both faced the mirror. Cupping his hands on her hips, he kissed her softly on the side of the neck. Caroline could feel Bryan's breath shorten and the pulsing of his erection against her lower back. From behind, he slipped his right hand between her thighs. Caroline felt herself warming momentarily with a blush before swatting his hand away.

"Stop!" she said firmly, stepping from the embrace.

"And what about Marian in all of this? Mrs. O'Byrne."

"She's...she's fragile at the moment. I'm waiting for the right time."

"I thought there was never a right time," she snapped back.

"Jesus, Caroline, stop messing about for just two minutes, will you? I'm serious. Myself and Marian are just...going through the motions."

She faced him square on.

"And I am serious. I can't be the other woman right now. Tonight's the beginning of something big for me. I can feel it."

"You will knock them dead."

"And what will you do?"

"Have another…drink," he shrugged.

*

The bar of the Palestine Hotel swirled around him. The live link had gone well. No cock-ups, but Bryan was increasingly starting to find that he could longer hold his customary few drinks, not like he used to. The Yank would be down soon-Audrey. He liked this young gun, her swagger, the energy she brought to the table. She was feisty, and *she could* go toe to toe with the best of them at the bar. For Bryan, those days were over. She joined him at the counter and in one movement ordered a drink and settled onto a bar stool.

"Jesus H Christ, Bryan. When are we going to get out of this fucking place and find out what's really going on," she snarled.

"Be my guest," he replied, making a sweeping gesture towards grandiose entrance of the hotel.

"You're not losing your bottle now, are you?" she goaded, sizing up the shot as it was placed on the counter.

"If you are not scared, you're already dead." Bryan twirled the remnants of his drink. "Taking risks will get you your head blown off."

"There's a job to be done," she retorted, finishing off her drink in one mouthful.

"Just keep your head down."

"Sorry, I can't do that," she countered, signaling for two more drinks.

Bryan laughed and shook his head. "You haven't being listening to a word I said."

Audrey handed him the shot glass. "Here, get that down the hatch. It will make you feel better about yourself. We need to head up north. That's where this thing will be won and lost. When the *Sulaimani's* engage. Bottoms up!"

Whatever he thought about yanks in general, Bryan had to concede that this girl had balls. Her streaked hair was tied back, but looked in need of the love and attention that this conflict couldn't offer, while the skin around her eyes looked weak. That's what had attracted him to Marian first. The fusion of grit and vulnerability. She was in full flow now about how the two of them needed to head north and work together to get the real story, but Bryan wasn't listening anymore. He was thinking of Marian and how it had all gone wrong.

*

They had met as teenagers, their first kiss at one of the school organised discos.

They had found a covert spot away from the prying eyes of the supervising teachers for an awkward moment, and that was it. Soon they were morphed into one-*Bryan and Marian.* Her parents were not as eager though, never really taking to him, so the wedding was a low-key affair in Rome, the young lovers alone with two random strangers as witnesses. They had never felt happier, their future stretching out before them. Happy until they became horribly unhappy. Happy until every conversation seemed to come back to the same day, the same blame game.

"We can't turn the fucking clock back, Marian, nobody can. Is that what you want to hear from me, for the umpteenth time, that I don't blame you."

"Everything is my fault eventually."

"What happened, Michael…was nobody's fault."

"I should have…"

Happy until they were torn apart by the same soul-searching week in, week out.

"And when the lifeguards laid him out, Bryan…he looked, just like he was sleeping. I never thought something so peaceful could cause so much pain."

"You have to try and let it go, hun. Get back to normal."

"Normal? Our child is gone, Bryan, your son."

"It was a tragic accident, Marian. Nobody to blame."

"And if you had been there?"

"I had a job to do, Marian. I just couldn't afford to spend a week lounging by the pool. I told you that at the time, but you went away anyway, and look where that got us."

"So, you do blame me so."

When she suggested counselling, he suggested Iraq. It was like a smart bomb going off in the kitchen.

"If I don't do it, someone else will. You know the drill."

"Iraq? And there's me thinking you wanted to make a go of it, of us, get back to normal. What was that bullshit about?"

"This is another chance for me to show them that I still have it."

"Suit yourself. You always did."

"Jesus Christ, Marian, you don't get it. My face doesn't fit anymore! Do you know what that means at my age?"

"And us, how is Iraq going to help that?"

*

Bryan needed another drink. "I hate this fucking place." There was despair in his voice as he signaled to the barman.

"So, what are you doing here so?" Audrey's eyes narrowed critically.

"I couldn't fucking tell you be honest," he answered as two more drinks arrived. "I thought I was coming to cover a war, well, that's a load of bollocks for starters. It's rooftop TV, that's what it is. You show me your rumour, and I'll show you mine."

"That's what I keep telling you," Audrey replied animatedly.

"Fucks sake, I mean they see a CNN dish, and it's significant fucking military activity."

"Exactly. That's why me and you need to take a wander around the north."

"Nobody cares," he sighed.

They touched glasses.

"I care," she answered with a flicker of a smile.

"News is a product," Bryan continued, "and if it's not making any money, you can forget about it. You can wander around the north all you like, but if David Beckham changes his hairstyle, you won't make the nine-o-clock news. Muslims, Catholics, Jews, who gives a shit," he finished resignedly.

"I do." There was conviction in her voice.

"I can't walk through an airport in my own country anymore without being practically stripped naked. I mean, I'm catching a connecting flight at JFK last fall and they take my nail clippers for Christ's sake. What am I going to do? Storm the cockpit and *take this plane to Barcelona, or I'll clip your nails*!"

Bryan threw his head back and smiled.

"It wasn't us flew those planes into the Twin Towers."

"And bombing the shit out of Iraq is going to solve all that." He spoke clearly.

"After 9/11 we needed something to focus our anger on."

"And Bin laden doesn't even get a mention anymore. It's a joke."

"That guy," she tapped her glass off the counter top for effect. "He didn't mean for those two buildings to come down, no way, he got lucky."

"And now Baghdad is paying the price."

She turned to face him.

"Freedom doesn't come cheap," she said earnestly.

"Is that what you're calling it now?"

Their gazes clashed and she took a sharp intake of breath.

"There was a girl I knew," she offered quietly, "from my hometown, and she got a late call-up to crew on that plane that hit the first tower." She dropped her gaze and returned to scan her glass. "It was a big thing for her, starting out, to get a long-haul flight like that. All the girls jump at those chances, kids trying to do something with their lives, going about their business.

Those guys cut their throats without a single thought. Where's the freedom in that?" She raised her head again, staring through Bryan.

"That's what this is about."

"Fuck it," he shrugged. "I don't know what I believe in anymore. At least with ye, there's no fucking grey with ye guys."

You had to hand it to the Americans, he thought to himself. *Everything black and white, straight down the middle.*

If only his own life could be so straightforward.

*

Caroline was on the up. The award ceremony was everything she had hoped it would be and more. The top brass making proper noises about her hosting a new Friday night magazine show and some serious flirting with the young Culture Minister, Enright. It wouldn't do either of their careers any harm, and then three weeks later, the icing on the cake – A VIP Style Award nomination for Ireland's best dressed female.

The dress had delivered.

She just needed to keep everything on an even keel now and not rock any boats.

Bryan would understand. He knew how the game worked.

"I just can't have any distractions, not at the moment. You know I'm busy with the pilot shows."

"All work and no play," Bryan teased, placing his arm firmly around her back and drawing her towards him. She resisted the final movement as he went to kiss her.

"I haven't got time for that now," she said dismissively, breaking from the embrace.

"The next few weeks are crucial for me. I'm this close to landing the Friday night slot, this close," she gestured with her thumb and index finger.

Bryan leaned back to prop himself against the kitchen work top. He watched her as she began to randomly tidy the living area of her apartment.

"You are excited, aren't you."

"What do think?" she answered flippantly. "This is a big deal for me."

"And do I get any mention in the corridors of power?"

Caroline stopped rearranging the displaced magazines and took a step back from the coffee table.

"They'll want someone in Baghdad when that blows."

"Jesus, Baghdad. They won't be able to give that away."

"Something to sink your teeth into."

"Are you serious?"

Caroline approached him at the counter top, leaned forward and kissed him gently on the forehead. She set her hand in his reassuringly.

"It would be good for you."

Bryan pulled his hand free. He crossed to the sink. There he poured himself a glass of water.

"Fucking Iraq."

*

Marian was incandescent.

"Don't you dare tell me to shut up," she raged.

"Just let me get a word in edgeways, so," he continued to harangue, but she was on an unrelenting attack now, eighteen months of hurt spilling forth between them.

"And you have your mind made up, haven't you, without even bothering to run it by me."

Bryan made a forlorn effort to comfort her. "Jesus calm down will you."

"Don't," she exclaimed, raising both arms to shield herself, "don't you touch me. I don't want you to touch me." Brian stepped back. "Ok, ok." There was genuine shock in his voice at her ferocity. From across the room, Marian composed herself.

"You haven't been there for me Bryan. Not when I wanted you, not how I needed you."

Bryan felt his throat tighten. "It hasn't been like that." He barely recognised his own voice. She looked at him indifferently before sitting tiredly.

"That's not fair," he continued.

"Fair...Iraq," she emitted a bewildered laugh. "It just can't go on. I can't go on." She sank her head into her hands.

"Twas you shut me out first, Marian"

The comment seemed to jolt her upright. "Oh, here we go, always my fault."

"Jesus, that's not what I'm saying."

None of this was how Bryan had envisaged coming clean. He had played this moment out over and over again on loop in his mind.

Was there ever a good time?

Her stoicism unnerved him.

"Do you love her?" she asked in a low, quiet voice.

Bryan cleared his throat, puffed out his cheeks and exhaled. She shook her head with all the contempt she could manage.

"And how long?" There was a sadness in her voice.

"Months," he answered. His voice level.

"I want you to leave."

"Now?"

"Get out, Bryan," she commanded. Her voice raised.

"It's after midnight, Marian. Where do you want me to go?"

*

Our man in Baghdad, Bryan O'Byrne joins us now with the latest. Caroline in studio here, Bryan, is there any concrete news on the fate of Saddam's sons who were targeted in that overnight attack?

Good evening Caroline. It is just after midnight here and yes, the American forces have tried to decapitate the Iraqi leadership in an attempt that saw the dropping of two four thousand pound bombs on a residential area of the city. However, British intelligence believes that Saddam's sons may have just left the building prior to the attack and the attempt has now widely believed to have failed, but there are some unconfirmed reports that the Americans believe something might have happened there.

And what's the situation like right now, Bryan?

Quite bizarre, in fact, Caroline. The Iraqi's are, in fact, claiming that they are chasing the American forces out of the city.

Is there any truth in that?

If there is, it has not been without a cost. The Iraqi hospitals I visited appear overwhelmed with civilian dead and injured. I estimated over twelve hundred dead between two of the hospitals I've seen.

So only a matter of time before the American forces topple the regime then?

What I will say Caroline is...

*

"It's over."

Bryan was wired, and Caroline had sensed it the moment she had buzzed him in. A coiled spring, unleashed.

After midnight.

He was talking in short, sharp bursts, barely stopping for air.

"For good this time."

And darting about the apartment, living, kitchen, living, kitchen.

"And Christ, do know what? It feels good to have it out in the open."

Unannounced.

Caroline felt lightheaded and the tightening of the knot in her stomach. She needed to process and take a step back from this vortex. Eventually, Bryan threw himself dramatically into the couch, arms and legs flailing before settling.

"And what do you think?" he asked.

Caroline moved her night-cap and magazine from where they had been set on the coffee table and placed them on the counter top. Returning, she picked up the remote control and shut the TV down.

"What do I think?" She repeated carefully.

"Yes, I did it, like I said I would."

"And are you sure, it's the right thing?"

Bryan crossed his legs, folded his arms behind his head and sank back comfortably.

"Never more definite about anything in my life."

"It's just a lot to take in," she added.

"Told her straight out."

"About me?"

"Straight up."

Caroline felt the blood drain from her face. "Jesus, Bryan," she groaned in panic, setting the remote control down on the glass TV stand with a bang.

"What?" he questioned, sitting forward quickly, cupping his hands under his chin.

"I told you I can't be doing this now," she answered with a burst of desperation.

"Look you are tired. We all are. We can talk about this in the morning."

Caroline straightened herself authoritatively. "You can't stay here, Bryan."

"What?"

"Not tonight."

"What do you mean I can't stay?" He looked puzzled.

"Jesus, Bryan, I see you what…once every other week and you come barging in here with some half-cocked story about leaving your wife, looking for a place to stay. It's one-o-clock in the morning, for fuck's sake!"

"I'm sorry. I should have rung, but you never answer the bloody thing anyway. That fucking voicemail."

Caroline steadied herself with her back to the window. The lights of late-night Dublin 4 twinkled behind her. "We need to sit down, Bryan. Talk properly."

"I'm all ears."

"Jesus Bryan."

"Try me."

"I'm…seeing someone." She spoke casually.

"What are you saying?"

"Someone else…new"

"What are you on about?" His voice was perplexed.

"Something more…stable."

"What's that supposed to mean?" he asked accusingly.

"A few weeks ago. We didn't mean it to happen."

"Who?"

"It doesn't matter who."

"I left my wife for you Caroline."

"And did I ever mention that, once, did l?"

"What?" Bryan's tone was filled with confusion now as he grappled to understand what was unfolding before him.

"I didn't ask you to do that," she repeated.

"Fucking who? Do I know him?" he flashed angrily.

"Noel…Noel Enright." Caroline's tone was controlled.

"The Green Party guy."

Caroline nodded.

"Minister for Culture, Noel Enright."

"Yes," she said quickly.

"Jesus Christ Caroline. He's only a fucking kid!"

Caroline remained steadfast. "He makes me feel good."

"And I don't?"

Slowly she walked to the counter top, took up her drinks glass, brought it to the sink and began to rinse it vigorously under the tap.

"What are you doing? Look at me," he barked sharply.

"It's less complicated," she replied clinically and turned once more to face him. Bryan stood up from the couch and began to pace the living area. "Don't tell me you're falling for that *golden couple* bullshit. You're too long in the tooth for that, Caroline."

"I'd like you to leave Bryan." There was no emotion in her voice, but Bryan didn't seem to be listening anymore. "Fucking the fucking minister. He'd do anything for a few extra votes!" he laughed loudly, coming to a stop at the counter top.

"Get out, Bryan," she said forcefully.

Bryan placed both his palms on the counter top and leaned forward. "You're some operator Caroline."

"Get the fuck out!"

This time he knew she meant business.

"Was that the plan, Caroline? Get me shipped out to Iraq for three months and ship the younger model in. Very fucking smart. Very smart."

*

"Smart bomb." Bryan threw his head back in frustration. "How can you even say that with a straight face?"

Audrey raised her eyebrows and took a moment. "You do," she answered in time.

"I tell it. I don't believe it. There's a difference." They both fell silent, the bar of the Palestine Hotel humming around them. Audrey folded her arms at the counter and shot him an interrogating look. "What are you thinking?"

"To be honest, I was thinking how can I cry for a nine-year-old Iraqi girl when I couldn't cry for my own son."

"You're one of the good guys," she said before raising herself from her seat, leaning across and kissing him on the cheek, "and I'm sure it wasn't like that." Bryan could feel the tender sweep of her lips as she sat again. He scanned her face. There *was* a fragility there. She had meant it.

One of the good guys.

"No, I let it come between us and now look at me, in this Godforsaken shithole."

"Fighting the good fight."

"I ran away," he added solemnly.

"From what?"

"My life."

"This is living."

Bryan turned to face her. "I don't want this. I'm a fucking phony. I want the sweet smell of success, the fame, the trappings, the pats on the back. The fucking cheese and wine."

"We all want a piece of that," she laughed in agreement, "but you reap what you sow. It's a no-brainer."

"I'm all sowed out, then." He sounded exhausted.

Audrey stood from her seat. "Come with me to the north, then, in the morning. I've got a ride up there at first light with an American advance patrol. Gonna sweep all the way through until they meet resistance. It will be the story of the war, and there will be enough in it for the both of us."

"I can't do it anymore"

"Last offer."

Bryan stood and the pair embraced.

A good man.

"Just be careful up there, ok."

They held each other apart for a moment before Bryan patted her gently. "Are we going to see each other again?"

"Depends on Saddam I guess," she smiled.

Bryan watched Audrey as she sashayed across the lobby of the hotel. He remembered how Marian had that swagger once.

Before.

At the lift, the doors glided open choreographically and she was gone.

He was a good man.

It was a long time since he had felt that, and back in his room he tried to make sense of it all. He *was* basically decent and it had taken this American youngster to make him look deep inside himself and see daylight. He lay on the bed, fighting the fitful drag of sleep. He needed to be clear-headed. He could make it work again with Marian. They both could. Yes, it would be a long way back for him, but he was prepared to put in the hard slog if that's what it took.

Get back to basics.

He had been a fucking idiot.

They had a shared history, good times and devastating days. That all counted for something. As he lay there, it all seemed to come together. Marian was essential to him. He became filled with yearning.

First thing in the morning.

He began to drift towards sleep, but fought it. First thing in the morning, he would set the ball in motion. Make the calls to get himself out of this kip, get himself home. That would show Marian he was serious. Sleep began to envelop him again. He was going to put the work in. For the first time in a long-time, he was going to do the right thing by his wife. He felt his eyelids getting heavy, but he was ready to allow that now. He began to drift. He thought of Caroline. She was probably in the *Ice Bar*, sipping with her new toy boy.

*

Caroline *had* been with Noel Enright when the news broke. She had stayed over after a night at the theatre and some fine dining in The Trocadero. She liked it there. They had booths. You could be public in private.

She hadn't time for shock. This was big and she needed to capture the mood of the nation. She knew she could deliver as the make-up artist applied some finishing touches and the floor manager counted her in. She thought of the last time they had spoken.

Dick.

She loved this job.

And the shocking news breaking today of the early morning bombing of The Palestine Hotel in central Iraq and the tragic confirmation that this daybreak attack has indeed claimed the life of our own internationally renowned news correspondent, Bryan O'Byrne. We can now go live to Baghdad, where freelance reporter Audrey Ruston is waiting with this report.

Caroline hoped this American rookie was up to the task and not some amateur hour sourced on last minute.com.

Caroline Casey, here in Dublin, Audrey. Can you fill in any more details of what in fact occurred at The Palestine Hotel?

Yes, I can hear you and I can confirm that just after seven-o-clock this morning a number of explosions rocked the Iraqi capital here as rockets slammed into The Palestine Hotel in the city centre and the Iraqi Oil Ministry. In fact, I myself had just checked out of the hotel moments earlier on route to the north with a U.S. Infantry Division when the rocket attack took place.

And can you shed any light on the immediate after-math of the attack?

Yes, I immediately made my way to the site and the impact scar of a direct hit was clearly visible on the front of the hotel, which as you know is used by western journalists. It was quite obvious that several people had been seriously injured and tragically very quickly con-firmed that Irish reporter Bryan O'Byrne, whom I had only spoken to as recently as last evening, was among the fatally injured.

And is it too early to say what went wrong or why The Palestine Hotel was targeted in this way?

At the moment, U.S. military sources are remaining tight-lipped and as of yet have not admitted responsibil-ity for the attack. There is some conjecture that a stray Iraqi surface-to-air missile may have inflicted the strike, but, and I must stress this is speculation at the moment, in the event of the more likely probability that this strike is the result of so-called American friendly fire, well then this attack could very well be the story of the war so far.

Caroline was impressed. This girl was good, very good. She needed to up her own game.

A lot of questions remaining to be answered, then?

Without a doubt, not least of which will be, if and when, as we expect, the American forces do, in fact, take responsibility for this tragedy. How could the use of the so-called smart bomb go so horribly wrong?

Thank you for that, Audrey. So, there we have it, confirmation of the tragic death of our esteemed colleague…

Caroline paused. This needed to be more personal, needed to go where the teleprompter couldn't bring her.

…But of course, more than that, a cherished husband and we extend our deepest sympathies to Marian at this most difficult time. A man whose kindness and generosity of spirit touched the lives of all who knew him, and who leaves behind a powerful journalistic legacy. A man who personified truth in a life dedicated to public service. His memory will forever remain in our hearts, and his spirit will continue to guide and inspire us every day.

On her monitor, Caroline could see the image the editor was using to close the bulletin. Pink sleeveless shirt, helmet, flak jacket, tanned, empty bladder and ready to rock and roll. The consummate professional. She knew she needed to deliver both a quiver and a tear to go out on a high. She stared down camera 1.

Ar dheis de go raibh a anam.

She could manage neither.

Parklife

Sully nudged the discarded sleeping bag with his foot. Behind it someone had scrawled: *Boycott RTE.* The writing was childlike, and it looked out of place. Sully turned to admire their own work:

> ### 2 Krooks
> ### TGB-Crew

The lettering all striking yellows with purple and black blocking. It had taken five painstaking nights to complete. *TGB-Crew* was Christian's idea. He had pinched it from some Youtube influencer he was following on Instagram. Sully had chosen a prime spot for it, right at the entrance to Fitzgerald's Park. No one could miss it. Growing up, Sully's grandfather, Pop, had always referred to Sully and Christian as "two proper little crooks," so that moniker had stuck. Sully was proud of the work:

> ### 2 Krooks
> ### TGB-Crew

Less than five feet away to his left, a crow dropped a piece of dried moss it had been gnawing and turned its head to look at Sully. They both stood their ground. Sully turned the sleeping bag over and the smell of dank piss cut through the fresh morning air. As the sleeping bag lapped over onto the grass the crow took flight, taking refuge on the iron frame of Daly's Bridge, the suspension bridge linking the park on Corks Southside with the Northside of the city. Down in the park, Sully thrust his hands in his pockets and stepped clear of the sleeping bag.

"Hey, give us a hand, will you? I'm stuck!" It was Christian. Sully could hear him, but couldn't see him.

"I'm stuck," he called again.

Sully looked towards the playground, fifty yards to his left. The City Council had recently installed a castle themed climbing maze for the young kids who visited the park with their parents, all ropes, ladders and chutes. At the base of the giant steel chute protruding from the main turret, Sully could just about make out a pair of Nike Air Max, toes pointed downwards.

Christian! What the fuck.

Sully crossed to the play area where his initial bemusement was confirmed, Christian wedged face down at the base of the steel chute.

"What are you doing, you Muppet," Sully laughed before stepping back to take it all in.

"Just drag me out will you! I can't breathe!" Christian's voice was filled with panic.

"Hang on."

"I can't hang on you langer."

Sully rummaged through the pocket of his hoodie and took out his phone. "Just hang on. I have to get this."

"What are you doing?"

Sully had his phone on record now and he crouched closer to his stricken friend.

"Have you anything to say for your followers?" he laughed wildly.

"Will you fuck off and just get me out of it!" Christian croaked back.

"Alright, alright, cool the jets."

Sully put away his phone slowly and deliberately before positioning himself at the base of the chute.

"Come on!" Christian urged once more.

Without warning Sully grabbed Christian by the ankles and yanked him from the chute unceremoniously. Sully staggered about the play area in mock exaggeration, laughing as Christian sat in a crumpled heap.

"Fuck you," Christian gasped for breath.

"What were you trying to do?" Sully asked, composing himself.

Christian was dusting himself down vigorously. "Face down," was all he could manage in reply, gesturing to the top of the turret. Sully laughed again, uncontrollably. Christian stood sheepishly. "Sausage."

"Who are you calling a sausage?" Sully challenged.

"You, ya chipmunk," Christian fired back, "and you can delete that video and all."

"I will yeah. And don't be calling me a sausage at all boy. Calling me a sausage, and you're the one getting done next month."

A young mother had arrived with two small children and eyed the two youths with suspicion. Sully and Christian took it as their cue to move away.

"It's better than community service," Christian mused, moving gingerly alongside Sully.

"Are you serious? Being locked up." Sully stopped.

"I'd prefer Oberstown than cleaning graves all day in Mahon."

Sully grabbed Christian in a playful headlock and ruffled his hair. "You're some spacer, do you know that!"

"Oberstown is a sound gaff," Christian replied, breaking free.

"Sure boy."

They continued to walk in unison, Christian scrolling his phone intently. At the gate they swung right, but not before Christian stopped to admire:

2 Krooks
TGB-Crew

"Class," he whistled to himself. "Come here, stand in," he called to Sully as he posed for a selfie in front of the mural. "Fuck that," Sully answered, and he continued with purpose towards the ramp which led onto Daly's Bridge. There he sat facing the river, ignoring Christian's cajoling. Out of the corner of his eye, he could see the crow.

Like old men.

"And I'm telling you it is," Christian continued randomly, sitting beside Sully. "Oberstown's A1."

"And how do you know?"

"I was told."

"Who told you?"

"Evan. He done nine months there."

"Evan is a spud, and you're a bigger spud to believe anything that comes out of his mouth."

Christian resumed scrolling his phone. "Fuck the Dubs. I'd wear my Cork City jersey going in there. Not a bother."

"And what about visits?" Sully asked thoughtfully.

"There wouldn't be any. My mam wouldn't have any way of getting up there."

"And your old man?"

Christian set the phone down and raised his head. "We have a barring order against that spud. The last time he came around our gaff there were shades, fire engines, ambulances, the lot. And the next time he sets foot inside the door, I'll reef him myself."

Sully laughed in agreement. "My old man went to the Lebanon and never came back, well, not to our gaff anyway."

"And where the fuck is he?"

"Shacked up with some old doll out in Blarney."

"What would you want to live out there for?"

The bridge hummed and swayed above them. An early morning *Just Eat* delivery cyclist was crossing swiftly. They both watched as the cyclist guided the bike off the bridge and freewheeled the bike down the ramp beside them. The crow swept onto the riverbank beneath them.

"Who the fuck orders food at this hour?" Christian whispered, but Sully was lost in the majesty of the bike as the female cyclist picked up speed and shot in the entrance to the park.

"Do you want a mountain bike?" Christian nudged Sully. "I know where we can get one easy."

Sully turned his attention back from the disappearing cyclist. "Fuck that. You won't be happy until you bring the shades snooping around my gaff. There's no scabby mountain bike worth that."

"I've somewhere to be," Christian said, standing abruptly.

"Where?"

"Just somewhere. Better than here, anyway," he continued, returning the phone to his pocket.

"Are you going to tell me or not?"

Christian's eyes darted both left and right, and he deftly pulled a flick knife from his pocket and activated the blade in one movement. "Have a look at that."

"Where did you get it?"

"On-line."

"Show it here," Sully said lowly, gesturing with his right hand, but Christian closed the knife skillfully and made to put in his pocket once more.

"Show us the thing will you and don't be acting the langer? What do you think I'm going to do?"

Christian activated the knife once more. "We could do *The Centra* on the back road," the black handle now flourishing in his hand.

"Are you off your game or what!"

"There's only one old doll there," Christian added excitedly, before pulling up his hood and brandishing the knife aggressively. "I could hold the beour while you grab the cash. Easy money boy."

"Stop waving that thing in my face and give it here for a look."

"Let's just do the gaff." Christian was bouncing on his feet now. "What's the problem? I'm getting done anyway."

"I'm not."

"Do you fancy her? Is that it?"

Sully threw him a look.

"The fiend is in love!" Christian mocked. "Suzie cum bum."

"Just fuck off, Christian...mog." Sully turned his back disdainfully.

"Who are you telling fuck off to?" Christian challenged and spun Sully around. "I'd cut you from ear to ear."

"Would you now?"

Sully sprang forward, grabbed Christian forcefully before disarming him and pinning him to the concrete in one swift movement. Sully had the knife now and was using his own body weight to hold Christian down.

"Cut me from here to here," he laughed, gesturing with the cold blade.

"My head, you langer! Lemme go!"

"What's up with you, boy!" Sully released the pressure and stood slowly. "You're a brave boy with a knife in your hand," he taunted.

"I was only messing. Now give us the knife."

"Make me," Sully spat as he ascended the ramp onto the bridge.

"Give me the knife now," Christian called after him as he clambered to his feet.

Sully stood on the bridge and dangled the knife over the edge high above the water. "Come and get it so."

Christian moved slowly up the ramp. "Stop fucking around, Sully." Christian's hand was outstretched within touching distance of Sully. "You're dead if you drop that, dead," he threatened.

"Dead?" Sully let out a sigh and allowed the knife slip from his grasp.

*

Sully stood at the midway point of the bridge. There was always a different perspective as the evening closed out. Sully preferred it, the river, framed by lush greenery, meandering slowly towards the city. The birds finished for the day.

Bonna Night would be different. It had been planned for ages and Christian was the main man. *Bonna Night would be bags of cans, shoulders, weed, fiends he didn't know and beours he couldn't care less about, all-in-one mad rush not to be the last one to jump from the bridge into the water below.*

Bridge shaking, whooping, hollering.

Not to take part would be a public disgracing there would be no coming back from. Sully knew that, but he also wasn't keen on breaking his neck just to impress a few old dolls.

Christian was stone mad.

For now, Sully let the tranquility consume him. Below him, the river bed was dark and murky. He scanned where the knife had plopped on entry before spinning into the darkness. Sully was still alive and allowed himself a smile.

Christian was always threatening to kill someone.

Sully raised his eyes. In the distance, he could just make out a grey-haired head protruding from the sleeping bag. *Boycott RTE* was in for an early night.

Messy.

On the riverbank, Pop had a catch. Sully watched him carefully remove the hook from the flapping fish and pop the fish into a hold-all. Pop beckoned for Sully to join him.

"It's a fine one. We'll get ten, twelve euro for it," Pop beamed. "The job is Oxo."

Sully watched him as he disassembled the rod diligently. "Could you use that trout rod for mackerel if you wanted?"

"Wouldn't be strong enough."

"Christian was saying you could if you just used a stronger gut like."

"That Muppet!" Pop stopped sharply. What would he know about fishing? They would make shite out of it in two minutes. "Do you want to fish mackerel?" he asked.

"He was saying they are breaking mad off Camden at high tide and there's money to be made."

"A load of bollocks," Pop answered, his jaw clenched. "You'll get nothing for them when they are breaking like that. Lucky to give them away. Christian says!" Pop nodded at Sully. "Let's pack up and head for the hills before Johnnie Bailiff spots us."

"I'd reef him first before I'd let him take a fish," Sully said adamantly as he began packing away the rest of the gear.

"There's no fish worth doing time for," Pop countered.

Bags packed, they ascended the ramp. A cold wind had lifted, and Sully pulled his jacket tight for protection.

"Were you ever lifted for anything back in the day, Pop?" he asked nonchalantly.

"Different times, young fella."

Halfway across the bridge Sully stopped, leaned over the side and balancing on his toes, scrutinised the water intently.

"Christian will be the first man in *Bonna Night*."

Pop stopped beside him. "That clown will get you killed one of these days if you are not careful."

"He's just…" Sully's voice drifted away as he straightened himself.

"Listen to me," Pop said steadily. "He's a head-banger, and all his family before him were head-bangers."

"He's my best friend," Sully asserted.

"I've seen lots of Christians in my time, and they all come to nothing."

"Two proper crooks Pop," Sully said lightly.

"I shouldn't have called ye that," Pop responded ruefully. "Your mother wasn't happy."

Sully turned to face his grandfather.

"You don't understand Pop. I'll have to try one. The whole place would think I'm windy if I didn't."

"And that's all that's bothering you, what people think?" Pop said disparagingly. "They are all head-bangers, boy and Christian is the biggest one!"

*

Christian was sitting astride a *Kawasaki Ninja*. The green and red of the bike's bodywork were glinting in the morning sun.

"Well, what do you think of her?" he asked.

Christian revved the bike continuously as all around them birds swooshed upwards in response, their din drowned out by the high-pitched growling of the *Kawasaki*, while down in the park, there was slight movement in the sleeping bag.

"Will you for fuck's sake keep it down?" Sully berated.

"What?" Christian answered vacantly, easing off the throttle.

"Where did you get her?"

"Took her from a student gaff on College Road last night." Christian's eyes were popping. "Got a chase off the shades and all," he added wildly.

"Give us a go off it."

"Later. Gonna plank it again for tonight. Take it out the straight road. Will get the ton plus out of her for sure. You should have been there."

"I was fishing."

"Fuck that. Opened her full throttle." Christian revved the bike again.

"We caught a beauty," Sully combatted.

"One! I'm telling you, river fishing is slow. Out of your head on a bike is the best bang in the world," Christian laughed manically.

"Were you stoned?"

"Goosed on me, mam's D5's."

"How many did you take?"

"If you are going to take one, you might as well take three or four," Christian reasoned as he shut the engine down. "Did you ever notice how the tunes really get pumping after a few yokes? One time we took a load of uppers with a load of gatt and went down to the bishop's gaff and set fire to his palm trees!" Christian chuckled energetically. "Some buzz! Tunes blaring on the stereo and the bishop fiend running around doing his nut with buckets of water!"

"You're a messy fiend," Sully said, shaking his head scornfully. "I'm not wasting my cash on that shit anymore."

"Do you want extra cash? I can get loads."

"Where?"

"The foreign students in town. They don't even know you're robbing them. Handbags, mobiles, the lot. We could go in along now if you want."

"Nah," Sully replied, ignoring the offer.

"The *Centra* then."

"Fuck off with the *Centra*."

"I was talking to her," Christian confided, leaning forward from the saddle. "Suzie, she said she'd meet you."

"Where did you see her?" Sully looked interested.

"I'm telling you straight, there was a big gang of beours bushing by the reza last night. She was in the middle of them."

"You're some sausage," Sully sniggered.

Christian sat back on the bike. "We could do the Parkview Stores instead so. There is only one old fiend on his own there," he offered, before restarting the ignition.

"No way!" Sully cut him off abruptly. "That old fiend is mad. Do remember the time Mousey went in there with a *Dunnes* bag over his head and two holes for eyes and that old fiend chased him up the road with a hammer?"

"That's just Mousey for you. The slow Muppet! That polio left his brain in the Mini that time. The night…" Christian's voice faded.

"Dean," Sully finished.

"Yeah, that night."

"Ye were haunted, Mousey didn't kill ye all."

"The car was in bits, and we had to reef the door off to drag Dean out and he just…died there on the grass." Christian's face was wistful.

"And the nurse ye hit?"

Christian edged the bike away from Sully. "I don't want to talk about it."

"The Echo was saying she had life-changing injuries. Pop heard she lost a leg."

"That's not my fault," Christian refuted staunchly. "If that mog Mousey hadn't clutched the Mini going into the bend, none of it would have happened." He patted the passenger seat of the *Kawasaki*. "Now are we going to do Parkview Stores or not?"

"Nah boy. What do I want robbing a scabby few euro from a ninety-year-old for?"

"So, you have better things to be doing?" Christian sneered, revving the bike one last time before take-off.

"I do."

*

Sully was edgy. He had agreed to meet Susan at seven. If Christian and the others found out, he would never live it down.

What are you worried about what people think, boy?
Fuck 'em.

Yes, he had spoken to her many times before, but not like this, properly and alone, just the two of them. Bang on seven she rounded the corner from Convent Avenue, hair in plats, grey tie-dye yoga pants matching crop top revealing a washboard mid-rift and eye-catching silver tummy piercing. White Aisics.

Normally, he would cut down across the back of the cricket club and through Fitzgerald's Park to make it to Daly's Bridge, but not to-night. To-night he could buy more time with her by strolling down Wellington Road and accessing the bridge on its Northside. There was no hurry.

As she bobbed alongside him, arms swinging, Sully felt uplifted. He wished he had the courage to take her by the hand. He wondered what that would feel like, to hold her, skin on skin. He had never touched a girl in that way, but his throat felt dry, and he couldn't muster the pluck needed for that move. As they crossed Daly's Bridge, Sully stole a sideways glance. She looked unreal, her eyes sparkling, and she smelled just gorgeous.

Strawberries.

Sully allowed a smile to spread across his face.

"What are you smiling at?" she questioned matter-of-factly.

"Nothing. I just am."

Sully checked her out once more as she settled down beside at the water's edge. Her pants left nothing to his imagination.

"I heard you were talking about me last night," Sully opened, his head tilted.

"Well, you heard wrong. You'd want to get yourself a hearing-aid."

"Who are you giving cheek to?" Sully tapped her playfully, Susan pushing him airily in response.

"That was Christian anyway! And do you believe everything you hear from that sausage?" She made to push him more forcefully, but Sully grabbed her arms instinctively to shield himself.

"Who are you pushing?" he taunted, continuing to hold her by the wrists.

"Lemme go," she shouted, squirming to escape Sully's grip. He pulled a face and released her.

"You polio." Susan rubbed her wrists vigorously. "And you nearly broke my chain and all." She began trying to straighten a delicate silver chain and pendant. "It's all tangled now, you Muppet." Sully leaned forward and took her by the shoulders. "Just sit still and let me fix it so." His voice subdued as he began working in silence to untangle the chain, their eyes averted.

"There," he said successfully.

"My grandmother gave me that before she passed away."

Sully allowed the pendant to sit in the palm of his hand, and he examined it closely.

"Savage," he complimented, running a finger tentatively along the pendant and chain, inadvertently brushing a freckle close to her breastbone. Sully allowed the pendant to slip on to her body before sitting back himself.

Strawberries.

He checked his phone.

"Give us a look at that?" Susan asked. Her voice filled with renewed energy. Sully handed her the phone casually.

"And where did you get a Galaxy S24?" she asked, turning the phone over in her hands precisely.

"Fifty euro."

"For an S24, SIM unblocked?"

"Off a Romanian fiend in town." Sully snatched the phone back. "Here, let me take your picture."

"No boy." Susan turned her head away from him.

"Why not?"

"I don't like getting pictures taken, that's all."

"I'll take the back of your head so," Sully laughed.

"Fuck off Sully," she fired brusquely.

"Ok," he agreed defensively, and she turned to face him again. He released the shutter.

Click-click.

"Will you stop, will you?" Susan covered her face with her hands, but it was too late.

"I'm only messing."

"Sausage."

Sully held the phone up for Susan to examine. "Do you want to see yourself?"

Susan grabbed for the phone. "Sully! Delete that," she demanded in exasperation, but Sully had jumped up lithely to evade her and backed out of reach.

"Delete it Sully, please!"

Sully waved the phone tauntingly in front of her. "Will you come gatting with me so *Bonna Night?*"

"I will. Now delete that."

"And we are all going to jump off the shaky bridge as well."

"What do you want me to do about it? Now delete it."

Sully stepped closer to Susan and showed her the phone screen:

Move 1 image to the Recycle bin?

Cancel   Move to Recycle bin

He allowed her to step forward and touch the screen.

*

The river was high. They had not had much to say for themselves. Even as they passed the museum in

Fitzgerald's Park, there was a stillness. Normally Pop would take that time to pass comment on the two busts, one of De Valera and the other of Collins, in their bronzed face-off in the courtyard. He never seemed to tire of explaining their bitter journey from allies to arch enemies. This morning, he seemed jaded, pre-occupied.

Sully also had a lot on his mind. He wanted to meet Susan again. The next time, he resolved not to be such a Muppet.

Messing with her head like that.

He had slept fitfully.

"The salmon will be running shortly, a day maybe hours," Pop said tiredly, leaning fatigued against the bridge's railings.

"You would never get them down here anymore, would you?"

"Jesus one time you would. When I was on the go, and I mean really on the go. It was more than just fishing then. I mean, you could eat them, make decent money. There was never a day wasted."

"And what about the bailiffs?"

"All we wanted to do was fish our own river. Bailiff's? Different sides of the same coin, and I learned that the hard way." Pop moved away from the side of the bridge towards the ramp leading to the waters-edge.

"What do you mean?" Sully asked, following him.

Pop turned to face his grandson. "Ah, it's not something I'm proud of. Forty years ago, now." There was a quiver in his voice. "We had a really big run after a week of non-stop rain. River flooding like mad, salmon running." Pop turned and pointed to a sheltered spot on the riverbank. "Just about there, the rain coming down in buckets, a driving wind, and you couldn't see your hand in front of your face," he hesitated.

Sully joined Pop at the top of the ramp. He could make out the barest nervous twitching in both his grandfather's hands. Pop leaned forward and placed both hands on the railings to compose himself.

"So, we had lamps' the same night, and we didn't give a shite about this heroic dash from the sea. There was no standing on ceremony. We were just raking them in."

"Ye must have cleaned up."

"We would have," Pop continued, his body tightening. "But the lamps gave us away."

"Shit," Sully chimed through gritted teeth. "Did ye leg it?"

"Should have, but I wanted to do the big man, acting the langer in front of the others. Struck him and I still regret it to this day." His voice shaking now.

"Fuck."

"Got three months for my trouble, so that's why I keep on at you. Don't go down that road. That's not for you. Are you listening to me?"

Sully paused to take it all in. Pop looked pale and drained. He contemplated the riverbank once more and tried to picture what it might have been like that night, a night more winter than summer.

"I am," he answered finally.

"Good. Do you want to come back later? We might catch a few." Pop's face softened.

"Not tonight. I've something on."

*

Pop had called it right. The fish *were* running. More fish than you could shake a stick at. Sully was lying prostrate at the waters-edge, sleeve rolled up, and his arm outstretched just above the rippling water. There, taking shelter under a ledge, draped in river weed, he could just make out the fin, the tail moving slightly.

"Shh," he gestured at Susan to be quiet. She was just too giddy for this type of work. Countless times, he had seen Pop perform this art. Once he himself had been close, but not quite perfecting the catch.

The one that got away.

Sully slid his hand deftly under the water and glided it into position. He was oblivious to everything else around him now with only the thumping of his own heart for company. Slowly Sully passed his upturned hand under the rock. He was inches from the fishtail now. He paused, perfectly still and then began the tickling motion so often demonstrated by his grandfather, first at the tail before skimming his finger along the belly. The fish remained trance-like and Sully could make out the gills. It was time for the grasp and wrench…

"Fuck!" His body flinched.

Susan had plunged her hand under his T-shirt. "Have you any tickles yourself!"

The fish darted away bullet-like and Sully watched in vain as it zigzagged across the river to disappear in the undergrowth on the opposite side.

The moment was gone, and now he found himself grappling vivaciously with Susan on the grass, their fits of laughter bursting through the night air. Soon he was on top of her and Sully could feel the shape of her body crushed beneath his. He pushed her hair back from her face. She looked radiant. He kissed her fleetingly on the lips and raised his head. She tasted of vanilla, and he felt a warmth course through his body.

Leonidas.

Susan cupped her hands at the back of his head.

"A proper one," she whispered suggestively.

He kissed her again.

*

Sully sat at the end of the bed, the mauve bath-towel folded neatly on his lap. It was *the good towel,* and his mother only ever took it from the hot press on special occasions. Downstairs, he could hear the hiss of the kettle coming to the boil again. More tea. The bush telegraph was in overdrive.

He thought of how Pop had remained resolute on Christian and now had been proved bang on the money. The shades had pulled Christian from a B.M.W. the previous evening, brought him to an emergency sitting of the court, and the judge put him straight to Oberstown.

Facebook was rife with it- *Wrote off a B.M.W in Bishopstown. Crashed into the side of a house and a Mercedes. Wrecked the gaff. Filmed himself. Out of his head on drink and yokes and when the shades arrived was asleep in the front of the B.M. The robbed till from Parkview Stores on the back seat.*

That prick will only get you in the height of it.

Only yesterday morning, as they left the park, Pop had admonished him once more.

He doesn't give a shite about you. I've seen loads of them lads in my time.

On their way out they had stopped at the new mural. Fifty yards from the sleeping bag, someone had created, a house-shaped cardboard box for a head on distinctive red shoulders. The face, sullen eyes and a downward turned mouth, the roof carrying the message in perfectly formed block lettering:

> *11754*
> *Homeless*
> *Increased by a 1/3 since 2022*
> *Raise wages*
> *Lower rents We got people out in tents!*

It had gone up overnight.

"Class," Sully acknowledged.

To their left *Boycott R.T.E.* was sitting on top of the sleeping bag, tufts of grey hair and a wispy beard. He looked forlorn.

"Some lads get awful breaks," Pop had said sagely.

Everything was Christian's fault with Pop these days.

Throughout the day Sully had tried to reconcile Pop's own revelation on the bridge with his incessant advice. His recurring thought was that it did not make him think any less of his grandfather.

I don't want you going down that road.

Pop had come clean man to man. He didn't have to do that and that's what Sully had wanted to tell him back at the house, but he was unable to find the words.

Christian's news had broken as he walked Susan home. It was the first night he had walked her through her estate, side by side hands thrust deep in his pockets. It was the next step on the road he wanted to continue on, proper boy and girlfriend, but he wasn't there yet. As he made his own way home, Sully's head was spinning from the day's events. Above all he didn't want Pop to feel undermined or diminished. Christian's arrest would bear that out. Sully would square that with Pop first thing in the morning.

It was 8.20am when his mother hammered on his bedroom door. He had checked the S24.

8.20 exactly.

And Sully knew he was gone the minute he clambered through the bathroom window. He was slumped awkwardly where he had fallen. Then the blur, the doctor helping Sully place him on the bed.

He wouldn't have suffered.

The undertaker would be along shortly. Sully stood and unfolded the towel before laying it meticulously along the body. For the first time in weeks, Pop did not look jaded.

*

The smoke from the bonfires draped on the Northside like a shroud. Intermittently as the winds changed, great swards of the smoke unfolded and set themselves free.

For all the world it appeared like huge balls of candy floss were wafting down towards the city. Everywhere stank of burn and the air felt muggy. Sully could feel it in his nostrils.

There would be no hi-jinks tonight, no plummeting from the shaky bridge into the murk. Instead, it would be an early night. He had the mass in the morning and his mother wanted him to say a few words about Pop.

The flowers were Susan's idea. The manager at the *Centra* had told her to choose whatever bouquet she fancied, wouldn't dream of taking a penny for them. She had chosen bright red roses. Sully had asked her to come. Yes, he wanted to clear his head, but he did not want to be alone. He had found the removal difficult, rows and rows of people sharing anecdotes he couldn't retain and the repeated mantra of how sorry everyone was.

No one had ever felt sorry for him in his life.

And the text from Christian:

> *Sorry to hear the news Sul*
> *Your Pop was sound RIP*
> *Crooks til we die!*

I shouldn't have called ye that.

Underfoot the bridge seemed uncharacteristically stable as Susan ceremonially handed him over the bouquet. Sully released it without fanfare. They both watched without speaking as the roses held their course in the centre of the river and meandered towards the city. As they bobbed from view, Sully turned away and stared into Fitzgerald's Park. The sleeping bag was gone and someone from the City Council had painted over *Boycott RTE*. Preparations were being made for the annual summer family festival. The first attempts at obliterating cardboard box man were also visible, eleven thousand plus homeless vanished from the public's consciousness at the swish of a brush.

TGB-Crew would be next on the hit-list.

Sully took it all in. Change was coming down the tracks and maybe that was a good thing. The city was reclaiming the park for its citizens. He turned to Susan.

"Maybe we should be heading. It's getting late," he suggested sensibly.

Susan held out her hand invitingly, and he took it in his.

The Parting Shot

Mary Lenehan packed a suitcase early one October morning in 1965, walked out the front door of The Stag, and never came back. The Coal Quay was awash with rumours. The general consensus was that she had a "touch of nerves", but the more exotic minority *knew for a fact* that she had run away with a sailor from one of the many ships that docked an array of cargo at Cork Port. Before leaving, she had left a neatly written note on the bedside locker of her sleeping daughter Carmel. Nothing was ever mentioned to Mary's husband Finbarr after, not about her disposition, the illicit affair or the parting shot to her sixteen-year-old daughter.

*

Finbarr was seriously pissed off and the further he walked away from Flower Lodge hadn't diminished his annoyance.

3-2! For fuck's sake.

He had just witnessed the unthinkable: his beloved *Hibs* blowing a two-goal lead to their bitterest rivals Waterford FC and, in doing so, hand *The Blues* from the sunny southeast the League of Ireland Championship for nineteen hundred and seventy-two.

In our own back yard!

There would be no living this down. As he rounded the corner quickly into Maylor Street he was met with further indignation. The Stag was closed.

What the fuck!

There for all to see through the opaque glass, the sign hung provocatively as clear as day: *Closed.* Finbarr looked at his watch in irritation.

Quarter past five. The Stag was never closed at quarter past five.

Finbarr hammered the door panel violently with both fists. There were no words required and no response from inside.

"Open up for fuck's sake," he muttered under his breath, quickly losing patience. In due course, he could make out the silhouette of his daughter Carmel on the other side of the door and the familiar sound of unlocking and bolts sliding.

"Not before time," he jibed as he squeezed past her, letting her complete the routine.

Carmel knew her father, knew that when he was in one of his moods' he was best humoured and not disturbed. She needed to speak with him, of that she had no doubt, to sort it out once and for all, but this evening was already looking bleak. The narrow pub was practically in darkness. At the counter on the left, a line of high timber stools were arranged straightly, while opposite them at lower tables red studded-leather stools. The leather covering had been Carmel's idea, and something

Finbarr had only agreed to after much conflict. Dotted along these lower table's candles flickered gloomily.

"And the electricity is still out," Finbarr confirmed to himself as he strode down the narrow aisleway. "This whole country is gone to the dogs."

"They're saying we should have it back by seven," Carmel replied nonchalantly as she returned behind the counter and rehung the set of keys beside the cash register. Finbarr removed his coat and hung it on the back of the last high stool. "Holding the whole country to ransom," he continued, sitting angrily. "And don't start me on that other shower! Two up they were!"

Finbarr maintained his flow before his daughter could answer. "And do you know what they did to top it off? Had a lap of honour before the game even started! We will never live that down with the Waterford crowd. 3-2!" he finished incredulously, putting his head in his hands.

"I hope you didn't go and make a show of yourself down there," Carmel said calmly, setting placemats along the counter top.

"So you would prefer me to let the Waterford lads out-shout us on our own turf."

"Just…," she allowed her voice to taper off.

"Fix me up a cup of tea there, so will you?" Finbarr drawled as he settled himself.

"And what will I make it on?"

"This country! The yanks are sending rockets to the moon, and we can't boil a kettle."

A lull descended between them and Carmel allowed it to flourish.

"Declan is calling later," she offered eventually.

"Is he now?"

"Can you not just be pleasant?"

Finbarr snorted in reply.

"Declan has no interest in this place, Dad," Carmel said bluntly.

"That's what you think," he fired back.

"He doesn't."

Finbarr considered his daughter's uncompromising reply for a moment. He gathered his thoughts.

"He'd like nothing better than to have his name over this door girl," he said confidently. "You just can't see it."

"If you must know," Carmel began hesitantly, but here father cut her off.

"What?" he commanded truculently.

"Nothing."

"Spit it out, girl."

Carmel knew it wasn't the time, and she held her counsel.

"No, not to-night."

"Fix me up a *Paddy* instead, so."

*

Slowly over time, after her mother's departure, Carmel became the real boss at The Stag. Although she had been too young to realise it, everything had changed for her that night also. Initially, it had been the cleaning which she had been happy to take on, but as the weeks gave way to months and there was no sign of a reappearance of her prodigal mother, soon there were barrels to be changed, deliveries to be received and bills to be met.

Her father, appearing to lose all interest, washed his hands of the place and soon the daily rationing of his *Paddy Whiskey* intake was added to her to-do list.

To an extent, she hadn't minded taking on the extra responsibilities, but her father was difficult and the washing of hands towards the business was on his terms.

He had, in fact, seriously baulked at her suggestion of re-covering the tatty stools with the deep red leather, not speaking to her for three days before reluctantly agreeing. He had also railed vehemently against putting a corrugated roof over the small backyard that led to the outside toilets.

"Nobody *ever* complained about going to the jacks in the rain," he argued, but she stood her ground and countered that The Stag needed to move with the times. When she then put forward the idea of possibly converting one of those same toilets to a *Ladies* he dismissed it out of hand.

"Women! What's the world coming to!" he declared, turning his nose up at the very thought of it. Carmel quickly resigned herself to defeat on this play for women's liberation. It was a step too far. She wasn't kidding herself. She had won some battles, yes, but the war was far from over.

For the first eighteen months following her mother's exit, Carmel had read herself to sleep. Every night she would unfold the note, their shared secret of a life her mother could not physically share with her daughter any longer, and read it studiously by the light of the same bedside locker where it had been placed. Even though she knew it by heart and every ink indentation, she poured over it faithfully. She bore no bitterness, but more a curiosity, trying to imagine what was going through her mother's mind as she sat pen in hand leading to the final sign-off without a trace of affection, just chilling advice.

Then, out of the blue, she met Declan at a dance in The Arcadia. Honest, hardworking, decent Declan and as they quickly became an item, her nigh-time ritual eased to a halt, the note lying unread for the last five years in its hiding place at the back of her wardrobe, unread until…

Her father.

From day one he had never warmed to Declan and Carmel had tried everything to initiate a thaw. Nothing worked. Even encouraging them to go and watch *Hibs* together had ended in disaster, her father claiming that Declan, "knew fuck all about football." When she had broached the subject of Declan's work ethic and his experience of the bar trade, tending bar as he did in The Western Star on Western Road, her father's riposte had been particularly cruel and cutting:

"We *own* the bar," he dismissed condescendingly.

Finally, Declan's proposal that it might be a good idea to hire in some ballad singers at the weekend from the burgeoning Cork folk scene in a bid to attract a younger clientele had driven Finbarr ballistic.

The Rubicon had been crossed.

Her father.

*

The first *Paddy* was almost gone when the stranger came through, tall, overcoat and a worse for wear blue and white crêpe paper hat tilted incongruously on his head. He took a seat and placed the hat on the counter, ruffling his hand through jet black hair.

"Was it down in Flower Lodge you were?" Finbarr asked abruptly.

Carmel bristled.

"Cracking game of ball," the stranger replied in a thick Waterford accent before removing his coat and hanging it on the back of his chair.

"Daylight robbery, more like! What about Morley handling it in the box? He practically picked the thing up and Carpenter that fool for a ref, waves play on. That's some achievement!"

The stranger laughed.

"What will you have?" Carmel interrupted, giving the counter where he sat a cursory wipe.

"I'll have a pint so," he answered warmly. He looked towards Finbarr.

"What are you having yourself?"

"Make it a *Paddy* so Carmel," Finbarr said grudgingly, gesturing with his glass.

The two men sat quietly as Carmel prepared the round and handed them their drinks.

"Here's to doing it all again next Sunday in the cup final. Will you travel up?" The stranger raised his glass.

Finbarr raised his tumbler half-heartedly in return. "After today's performance? Wouldn't cross the road to see either of them."

Carmel raised her eyebrows in surprise. "Don't take any notice of my father there. He'd watch two flies going up a wall!"

Finbarr threw the drink back in one gulp.

"Not anymore," he cracked back pointedly.

*

Finbarr and Mary *had* traipsed all over the country following *HIbs* and Cork Athletic before that. Their love of football was the one thing that they had in common. It had brought them together and Mary really *knew* her football. She held her own comfortably in the various bar conversations that regularly broke out on all matters football.

"Fellas can talk some awful shite with drink in them," she often joked and Finbarr loved that about Mary, her ability to connect, no airs and graces. It gave him great satisfaction to see her in action, keeping everyone in check.

As a young couple, they had gone to see *Athletic* beat Waterford in the cup final of 1941. Finbarr had never forgotten any detail of the day. They had travelled to Dublin in his father's old *Ford*, foot-loose and fancy-free. After the game, they had gone back to their hotel at the Four Courts. The Waterford players were staying there, and both Finbarr and Mary had drinks with them at the bar. It was one of the great days.

Before Carmel was born.

*

It was New Year's Eve when Carmel returned to the back of the wardrobe. She was a frisson of unexplained nervous energy as she took the note from its hiding place and sat on the bed.

Why tonight of all nights she couldn't explain, but the pull to read her mother's farewell words once more had been building gradually over the Christmas period. It had crept up on her, a combination of her father and Declan's plans. She had gone through this ritual on countless occasions, but time had dulled her memory as to the exact contents. As she unfolded the sheet delicately, it was as if she was doing so for the first time. Now on the threshold of another year, her mother's voice did strike a chord and much of what Carmel had failed to grasp as her sixteen-year-old-self appeared clearer.

For the first time, she could sense the plaintiveness of tone as her mother asked for Carmel to *"hopefully find a way"* to understand the decision she was making. The resignation behind her mother's *"choice"* to live the life she had led for over twenty years also crystallised, and reading where she had written she couldn't *"do that anymore"* now brought a lump to the back of Carmel's throat.

Carmel's hands were shaking, and she felt the tears welling up. Slowly, she ran her finger over the last line. She thought of her mother writing that line, how that must have felt. She began to cry uncontrollably. She allowed the note to slip from her hands. She thought of her father. She thought of Declan. The tears flowed.

*

Declan arrived at The Stag just after seven. He had stayed in Blackrock after the match drowning his sorrows with a band of *Hibs* supporters who couldn't face the walk back into town in the immediate aftermath of the game. That would have been too painful, the mingling, the slagging, the banter. It had been a gut-wrenching defeat and the prospect of facing the same opposition in the following weekends cup final did not inspire confidence. However, soon the pints were having their desired effect and slowly the post-match dejection eased.

Declan felt unsteady as he finally made his way back into the city. There was a lot to mull over, to make sense of. Carmel had been trying her best to iron it out with her father over the last few months, but Finbarr was obstinate. It really was time to clear the air. Declan did not like the way Finbarr treated her, spoke down to her. She really put up for a lot, and Declan felt a troubled joylessness in her behaviour of late. That's why what he was proposing simply *had* to work. The alternative could not be countenanced. Declan also knew there would be no easy way to broach this with Finbarr.

Finbarr would definitely be in one, he thought to himself as he crossed into Maylor Street. He didn't do defeats, taking them way more personal than Declan and the younger *Hibs* supporters. For Finbarr, it was always a matter of life and death. He also knew that Carmel would be trying to placate him. Ease him off the *Paddy.* Carmel *was* the business. Everyone could see that. Everyone except her father. She had even tried to explain that Declan had no interest and was no threat to the business. Declan was happy at The Western Star, but ploughed every penny he could muster into his plan. The bar, any bar, was not his future.

Carmel and Declan had discussed that. At first, he had met resistance from her, but of late there had been a softening of Carmel's stance, especially since Christmas and now…

The Stag would be quiet. The *Hibs* lads too sick with defeat for a night in the pub and the Waterford crowd would be heading down home. The timing might never be better.

Declan placed his hand on the door. He braced himself.

*

Carmel was standing wiping glasses. She looked strained. At the counter sat some blow-in and down the end of the bar, Finbarr with a big bull's head on him. Declan needed air, needed to be somewhere else, anywhere else.

"How is the form?" he said quietly to Carmel, nodding faintly in Finbarr's direction.

"The match has him cranky," she shrugged.

"What did she say there?" Finbarr asked defensively.

"Just looking for a quiet drink after the game, Finbarr, that's all," Declan answered strongly.

"Let me look after it so," the stranger interjected, taking his wallet from his pocket.

"It's fine." Declan waved the gesture away. "I was thinking we might slip out for an hour," he said, addressing Carmel directly. "Can he not look after the place?" Carmel moved from behind the counter.

"We were thinking of stepping out there for a bit," she said in a low controlled voice before placing the dish-cloth on the counter where her father sat. "Will you be ok to hold the fort?"

"Isn't it great to be able to swan in and out when you feel like it." Finbarr's voice grated.

The stranger made to stand up. "Maybe I should head for the hills also."

"You will do no such thing," Finbarr argued. "You're my guest here." He took his place behind the counter.

"I'll fix up two *Paddy's*. And will you have one for the road yourself?" he added sarcastically for Declan.

"No."

"Jesus, we know who wears the trousers!" Finbarr laughed as he fixed the two drinks.

Declan felt an anger rise within him and knew he needed to control it.

"Ah you're drunk Finbarr. Go way and have a lie down for yourself." Declan turned from the counter indifferently. He placed his hand gently on Carmel's shoulder to lead her towards the door.

"Good to meet you," he nodded at the stranger.

"Likewise."

"Don't walk away from me, you little scut. I'll lie you down if I come out to you!" Finbarr rose his voice angrily.

"Don't mind him," Carmel said under her breath, gripping Declan tightly.

"Don't make me laugh," Declan said over his shoulder.

"That's it, go on. Clear off the pair of ye. I'll run my own pub, thank you very much."

Declan wheeled towards the counter brusquely. "Fuck off, Finbarr. And stick this place up your hole while you are at it."

Finbarr laughed exaggeratedly as he finished preparing the drinks. "See Carmel. See what did I tell you? He does want to get his paws on this place. You just can't see it!"

Declan was facing Finbarr now.

"You're an eejit Finbarr, do you know that? A think fucking ignoramus."

"And is that all you have to say for yourself?" Finbarr asked, setting the two drinks down on the counter with a flourish. "Well piss off out the door so. You're barred!"

The Stag fell still.

"Are you coming or what?" Declan coaxed Carmel, but she was rooted to the spot where she stood. She stepped forward to the counter before speaking.

"In fact," There was a slight quaver in her voice so she stopped, took a very deliberate slow breath and composed herself.

"In fact, we do have something to say."

It wasn't how Carmel had imagined it would be the countless times she had rehearsed it. In her mind she had envisaged the three of them maybe sitting after closing time, night-caps in hand, and Carmel formally announcing that Declan had something they both would like to chat with Finbarr about. In that version of events Finbarr would be calm and reasonable, fully under-standing of why herself and Declan would want to make a new life for themselves in south Boston. She had liked to think that as Declan meticulously unveiled their plan that there would have been some tears on everyone's part, but that her father would ultimately accept that it was all for the best. Some nights she imagined her father admitting with regret that her mother had indeed run The Stag for twenty years before it finally ran her. In all her imaginings the conversation would end with more tears and hugs, her father recon-ciling himself with this new future as she had done her-self since Christmas. In none of her musings was her mother's final salvo ever mentioned.

At her most upbeat she imagined her father immedi-ately making plans to put The Stag on a more sound business footing, perhaps renting it or even placing the premises on the market for sale allowing himself the opportunity of purchasing a nice home in the city and affording him the time to visit the young couple state-side on occasion. What she couldn't explain to herself was why she had chosen this moment to share both their dreams with her father, or maybe it had chosen her. Maybe she was finally taking the advice, her moth-er had written all those years ago.

You will also have to do the same as me some day

She had read that closing line repeatedly.

And only when that time comes will you fully understand that choice.

What she had not foreseen was the barrage of rage and derision in her father's reaction. "Boston my arse!"

And only when that time comes...fully understand.

Declan had stood in silence, but he could sort the rest. She wasn't returning. He could come in a day or two and collect what few belongings she needed. The tickets were bought. There was no turning back, not now. She would leave the note. That mantle had been passed on. Now it was her parting shot, and she hoped that someday, when he least expected it, her father might find it. Some day when herself and Declan were just another one of the loving couples strolling hand in hand on the Harbourwalk.

"Take me out of here," she said evenly, and as Declan took her by the hand, opening the door to allow her through she was determined. She was never setting foot in The Stag again.

*

The door swung shut.

"She'll be back in an hour, that one," Finbarr grunted.

"Families, eh," the stranger concurred.

"She was trouble from day one that girl and the wife, Mary...she was never the same after. Went into herself, a downward spiral. The doctor said it was natural that it would pass, but it never did. She lost interest. Every-thing changed," Finbarr gestured despairingly.

"You'd be a foolish man to let it lie like that. You'll regret it," the stranger answered cooly.

"I'll be the judge of that."

"I lost someone once," the stranger continued, stony faced. "Let a stubborn streak get the better of me. Never laid eyes on her again. A row. A thing of nothing. To be honest, I don't even remember what it was about now."

"I asked Mary to marry me in The Four Courts Hotel. We had just won the cup, and it seemed like the perfect thing to do. Her face lit up like a Christmas cracker, and do you know what? I don't think I ever saw her so hap-py again."

Neither of the men spoke.

"This time I am off," the stranger said, lightly break-ing the silence. He stood to put on his coat. "I might see you at the cup final."

"Indeed, you won't," Finarr said defiantly, "and I never caught your name."

"I never gave it," the stranger grinned. He pushed the door open, saluted, and he was gone.

They were always a clannish auld shower, Finbarr thought to himself as the door closed lightly. He began to tidy the counter top. He picked up the stranger's crêpe hat. *Up the blues,* scrunched it with relish and fired it towards the bin. *Got it in one!* He allowed him-self a smile as the lights flickered back into action.

"Things are looking up," he said aloud to himself.

He would go down to the Quarry on Tuesday night and see how *Hibs* were shaping up in training. *You never know* he thought to himself.

They might do those bastards in the cup yet!

A Slice of Good Fortune

Pigeon always planned their nightly entrance to Bal-lyphehane Park with military precision, arriving at quarter to ten through the south gate, just before clos-ing, when the checks had been done, and then it was a straightforward set up for bed under the sycamore tree at the back of the grotto. It was a secluded spot tucked away in the corner of the park with only one access point and their backs then sheltered by the grassy mound that sloped from ground level to the top of the grotto, a safe place, a place where himself and Teresa could keep themselves out of sight of prying eyes and the earshot of the local teenagers who sometimes scaled the park railings to go late night drinking.

Most nights Teresa did offer a token resistance, why did they keep returning to this Godforsaken hole and not try and secure a couple of beds at one of the shelters in the city? But Pigeon's reasoning was always equally consistent, nobody was forcing her to come, and the shelters could at times be hostile and unforgiving places. He preferred this oasis, this place where he could regroup. Teresa constantly reminded Pigeon dur-ing these clashes that her father had clerked at R&H

Hall and that the entire O'Neill family had been people of note.

"Pencil pushers!" Pigeon would mock in return, turning up his nose in disdain.

And while Pigeon would never admit it, Teresa was different and would have probably have gone under long go without him. They both knew that.

"Sleeping in a big fancy bed won't change your life you know," he'd sigh, settling himself into his sleeping bag.

And when she'd ask, "And you'd know that for a fact?"

He'd answer decisively, "I would."

Pigeon was proud of his time on construction sites across England through-out the seventies, proud, as he put it, that he had "helped build that place." In moments of reflection, he blamed everything on 1986, returning as he did to nurse his ailing mother, her death and the subsequent economic downturn. He had come home at the wrong time. Teresa, for her part, was not willing to discuss her life's woes, not even to Pigeon. Something had happened, and her family pushing her away was the limit of the insight she shared.

They had broken the first golden rule of AA, hooking up as they did at a meeting in the city and then forming a relationship of sorts. It was frowned upon by the sponsors and the remaining twelve steps were never negotiated. Teresa had attended those first few meetings with good intentions, but just didn't want to put the work in, while Pigeon had only attended that first evening out of boredom, "looking for somewhere to escape out of the cold," as he put it.

As the summer dusk dimmed into darkness, Teresa knew the drill, Pigeon always taking a few moments in prayer. If at that moment she ever made to speak, he would signal with his hand that he was in meditative mode and was not to be interrupted. It was the habit of a lifetime for Pigeon, and not something he was ashamed of. When the moment passed, it was then something he would make light of. "I said one for you and that our fortunes might improve." Of late, Teresa had found herself also using this time to contemplate on her own life. Regularly her thoughts had been leading to her sister in Waterford. They had lost contact over the years. She wondered about reconnecting and how that might play out. If the time did come, she didn't want any handouts, she would be adamant about that, merely a fresh start with family.

"I was thinking again about my sister," she mused aloud. "The girl in Waterford."

Pigeon sat upright, placed his index finger over his lips and gestured for silence.

"You're not even…"

"Shh," he cut her off, gesturing once more.

Pigeon unzipped his sleeping bag slowly and deliberately before getting to his feet in slow motion. He crouched low. Signaling with his thumb, he crawled up the grassy mound at the rear of the grotto that led to the top. Once there, he peered over the rim.

There was movement below.

*

Both Pa and Ronnie were seriously out of puff. The *Deliveroo* cyclist had battled hard to hold on to his electric bike. At one point in the struggle, he had even managed to get Pa in a headlock and if it wasn't for Ronnie's superior strength, Pa shuddered to think what might have happened. Pa had found himself losing consciousness just before Ronnie had dragged the cyclist to the ground and flailed kicks into his prone body. Pa had even felt a smidgeon of respect for their fallen adversary as he dragged himself to his feet and chased them in vain as they made good their getaway. Pa had clung on to Ronnie's mid-rift for dear life on the back of the machine as Ronnie darted in and out of traffic at full pelt, oblivious to honking horns and dodging pedestrians. The prize was theirs.

"She's an animal of a thing," Ronnie smiled elatedly.

"We'll get six hundred euro for her," Pa agreed, stepping from the back unsteadily.

"Five of that is mine," Ronnie quipped angrily, alighting and resting the bike against the kneeling statue of St. Bernadette Soubirous.

O God, today I will do my best. My very best.

"What the fuck. You said fifty-fifty," Pa pleaded.

"And the fiend beating you round the place. Go way and don't be annoying me," Ronnie argued, circling the bike where it stood. "You can have a hundred or fuck off."

"Ok, so," Pa muttered sullenly.

"Now are you going to give me a hand with this or not. We'll plank it here for the night and collect it in the morning."

*

Pigeon could feel his heart racing. He stretched forward as far as he deemed safe, conscious of striking a balance between taking it all in, not been seen by the boys and the risk of plummeting the sixty feet below. He was getting too old for this. As he stained forward, he could make out two youths manipulating a large electric bike at the entrance to the grotto's cave. The stronger looking of the two had the bikes front and was forcing it behind the statue of the Virgin Mary. He was obviously in charge. Occasionally, the bike clanged the base of the statue, and Pigeon could clearly make out this youth chastising his partner at the rear of the bike. Finally, the youths disappeared from view into the mouth of the cave and Pigeon jumped with a start. Teresa was beside him now. She made to speak, but he placed his hand across her mouth. Teresa shook it away in angry silence and as she pulled herself alongside him. Pigeon thought better of stopping her.

"Don't breathe a word," he hissed, his mouth twitching.

They could hear faint sounds from the recess of the grotto below before all fell quiet. Both Pigeon and Teresa shot their heads back as the two youths re-emerged. Pigeon lifted his head ever so slightly, gesturing for Teresa to remain prone on the grass where she lay. He trained his eyes on the pair as they crossed the park and bunked the railings on the eastern side. He continued to motion for silence as he watched them disappear into the summer night.

*

"Didn't I tell you this place would turn up trumps!" Pigeon was positively glowing with delight as himself and Teresa stood at the mouth of the grotto. He lunged enthusiastically beyond the statue of the Virgin Mary and began wrestling frantically with the bicycle.

"Come here to me my beauty!" he proclaimed victoriously as he emerged from the dark recess breathing heavily and leading the prize possession.

"Da da!" He made a flamboyant sweeping gesture to reveal the bike fully to Teresa. "What do you think of that?"

"Do you think it's wise…to cross those two young fellas," she offered reluctantly.

"They're hardly going to report it stolen now are they!" Pigeon scoffed. "Finders' keepers, I say."

Teresa shuffled and blessed herself.

O God, today I will do my best. My very best.

"I don't know Pigeon. That's all I'm saying."

"It's our good fortune to be in the right place at the right time." Pigeon could hardly contain himself with the excitement of it all. He patted the saddle. "Sit up there now, girl, and I'll give you a right good spin!"

"Stop it, Pigeon. This isn't the time for your auld codacting."

Teresa was right. It was time to make themselves scarce. The morning wouldn't be pretty when those two buckos returned and Pigeon knew it. They should gather up their stuff. There was still time to get one of the better pitches in the city centre for the night, a nice sheltered doorway along the mall. In the morning, he knew where he could cash in their new-found wealth for a couple of hundred euro. Tomorrow would be a brighter day.

*

"Fuck!!"

Ronnie was apoplectic.

"What?"

"Fuck!"

"Calm down."

"I am fucking calm!" Ronnie roared back at Pa. He was rocking back and forth in disbelief, head in hands, at the mouth of the grotto's cave. "The bike, that's what. Someone has lifted it," he barked, barging his way back into the recess. He kicked the air in despair.

"What do you mean someone's lifted it?"

Ronnie re-emerged from the cave, grabbed Pa forcefully and dragged him inside.

"Look. The bike. It's gone." He steered Pa around the cave by the scruff of the neck before releasing him with a violent push.

"It can't be," Pa blurted, his eyes wide in disbelief.

"Well, it is and when I find out who did it, I'll…" Ronnie's voice shrunk, and he stepped back out into the daylight.

"Just think for a minute," Pa argued, but Ronnie wasn't listening anymore. He paced the grotto and stifled a laugh.

"You little pussy," he said finally, pointing at Pa. There was an angry shake in his voice.

"What?"

"You're fucking…" Ronnie roared through gritted teeth, and he began to beat himself about the forehead.

"I don't know what you're on about."

"Don't give me that shit," Ronnie accused. "You little snake. I show you my stash and this is how you repay me."

Ronnie lunged at Pa knocking him to the ground, the force of the blow also causing Ronnie to lose his footing. Both youths crashed in to the kneeling statue of St. Bernadette, with Pa using the momentum to clamber to his feet and scramble free.

"I haven't got your fucking bike," he screamed painfully.

"I'm not messing about, fiend," Ronnie answered as he righted himself. His voice was low and hard, his eyes narrowed in anger.

*

Pa examined himself carefully. His heart was still pounding, his body churning. That robbery had been too close for comfort. The bruises and scrapes where the cyclist had gripped him were dark and highly visible. Pa touched the wounds. He was sore. The sensation of struggling for breath flowed through him again. He stepped from the mirror. He couldn't risk that happening again. And for what?

A hundred euro.

He needed to give himself an edge. He needed more, to survive. It was the way of the world. His mind was made up. Starting in the morning he would never be disadvantaged again. Ronnie had saved him and then made shit of him.

*

"I don't want to be fighting Ronnie," Pa said warily, slipping the knife from his pocket.

"What the fuck is that!" Ronnie laughed derisively. Pa was tapping the knife nervously against his leg.

Tap...tap...tap.

"Can we not just forget about it?" Pa shivered.

"Can't do that." Ronnie shook his head and stepped forward. "What are you going to do? Stab me in the neck, is it?"

"Don't make me."

"Use it or lose it," Ronnie challenged fearlessly, but before he could set himself properly Pa's athletic forward lunge caught him completely off-guard. Ronnie felt a short, sharp piercing pain in his jugular and clasped his hand around it instinctively.

"Think you're a big boy now," he gasped, staggering to face Pa, but Pa was galloping into the distance now, knife in hand. Bolting as his accomplice keeled before the feet of Our Lady.

*

Teresa had felt uncomfortable through-out the night, but not Pigeon. He had slept like a log, bicycle wedged in-side him. Those two scumbags hadn't cost him a thought.

"What goes around, comes around," he reassured, and he would split the spoils evenly, knowing that this would serve to placate her even further.

And Teresa did feel improved with a solid wedge of 300 euro safely secured deep down in her inside pocket. Pigeon would want to make a bee-line to the off-li-cence, and she would go through the motions with that, but her mind was racked. She had enough now to make that trip to Waterford, secure a place to stay for a night or two, make contact.

No handouts.

A new chapter. She wouldn't tell Pigeon, not today, she would let him bask in the glory of his slice of good fortune. He was right. She had no business letting her apprehensions get the better of her. Those two gougers were probably out already terrorising some other poor misfortunate. They would get their comeuppance even-tually. She made a sign of the cross.

O God, today I will do my best. My very best.

This *was* a good day.

The Backbenchers

The Lough Cork

In all my time I never actually saw Paul sitting on the bench. He always stood, back left, Tom central and Seamus back right. That didn't get a mention in the church today, and they gave him the full military honours to be fair. Blue and gold Barrs flag followed by a guard of honour. I could only think of Mossie as the coffin passed me down the aisle. If a Mossie in his prime had seen that carry on.

"Paul, shur that fella didn't know a football from a sliothar. None of the Buckley's ever played anything. Jesus wept. Paul? Paul couldn't get out of his own way!"

Paul was also a staunch Fine Gaeler, a Peter Barry man, canvassed for him at election time, a loyal footsoldier which didn't sit well with Mossie either, or Seamus. Seamus the biggest ball-hopper of the lot of us.

"Varadker! Foe fucks sake Paul."

And they'd be off.

"You're some man to talk, Seamus. Your crowd have done nothing for Cork boy, nothing. Two dummies in The Dail. Shur didn't they let The North Infirmary close that time!"

Tom would be standing between them keeping them at arms-length, like a boxing referee, sometimes dropping a little bomb of his own into the mix and then the both of them would turn on him.

"You have no say Tom boy. You don't exercise your franchise. People died for that."

Tom, the first to go. A slow horrible death. We never mentioned it again after.

Mossie sat front and central like the captain of a football team, and he always brought a bag of bread for the swans. We used to kill him over it. Tom especially, he was a mine of random information.

"Mossie, do you know that bread is a killer? Rots their guts big-time so it does, botulism, riddles them with it."

And Mossie continuing to feed them anyway, drawing Tom out even further.

"I'm telling you, it affects their digestive tracts. I saw it in the paper."

Mossie, not having a bar of it.

"Will you go way out of it? They put all kinds of shite in The Echo now just to sell papers. I have been feeding swans all my life, and what harm has it ever done?"

Dan would be sitting front right, not saying much, taking it all in. Always measured Dan.

"I don't want to ruffle any feathers now, Mossie, but did you ever consider…lettuce or broccoli?"

"I didn't. How would you feel if you came in some night and your Mary threw you up a feed of broccoli? Give me strength!"

Tom got sick shortly after, nothing noticeable, not at first, just a bit quieter and a bit shorter with the two boys, Seamus and Paul.

Tom and Paul had worked together in Fords and when it closed, everything gone. Men in their fifties with families to feed. That was hard, especially for Paul. He had a supervisor job with a bit of status and then nothing. Nobody ever said it, not out here, not amongst us, but it was said in town.

"What did the merchant prince do for him in his hour of need?"

Canvassed for him and all.

"Politicians, they're all the bloody same them fellas," Mossie spat, venomously at the time. *"Only in it for what they can get out of it themselves. No interest in the ordinary workers."*

All the while Dan staying out of it, non-committal, being Dan.

We never saw Dan again after COVID. He did come out one of the mornings you could travel the 5k, but it didn't feel right, standing apart like that. Tom reckoned there was more to Dan's vanishing than social distancing, reckoned someone had said something he finally took umbrage with. We never heard different and didn't make the effort to find out. None of us did. Maybe I should have. I certainly could have. I spent thirty years on the job, a year in Dublin starting off, a few years in Macroom and then twenty years in The Bridewell. I could have made a phone call at the very least, but I suppose I did not want to upset the apple-cart. Dan had his reasons and I thought it was best to let sleeping dogs lie.

Anyways it was Mossie I knew the best, from back in the day, fishing by The Lough, carp mostly and then after I retired, I met him out there again one morning. We had a brief chat and one thing led to another and soon, without even noticing it, I was spending three mornings a week down there putting the world to right. On retirement my intentions had been to get something cushy, just to get me out of the house, so I did a driving instructor course and passed with flying colours. Two weeks into it, I collected this Indian nurse in the South-side, and she plonks her two kids in the back seat because she couldn't afford a babysitter. I mean, what was I supposed to do? Halfway round the magic round-about, her little fella gets the gawk all over the back seat. Projectile. I jacked it in that Friday. I didn't need the hassle.

Seamus got a right kick out of that before he started to drift away himself about eighteen months ago. I met him in The Marina Market for a coffee one morning, and we talked about making it a regular thing, knowing we never would. He had got himself a Jack Russell and had taken to walking it around The Atlantic Pond, said I should do the same. Herself was having none of it, blew a fit, and she was well within her rights. She would have ended up walking it, minding it. Me and a Jack Russell. Wouldn't I look sweet?

Paul, for his part, he kept coming to the bitter end even when his family wanted to put him in a home, and he reduced to a slow shuffle on his walker. The last time I saw him was after mass in The Lough Church one Saturday. He had a cut on his nose from a fall, but was in good spirits. That was Paul all out. He asked me down to The Lough for old-time's sake, but I had somewhere to be. Told him I'd catch him next time. That's the one thing I regret.

I went to see Mossie yesterday to tell him about Paul. He is above in Mount Pleasant, a shell of what he was, the mind gone. It took a hold suddenly, a cruel bastard of a disease, and he went downhill quickly. It was really hard to fathom how someone so strong-willed, someone we all listened to, the leader of the pack so to speak, would never hold a normal conversation again. The others fell away, but not me. I wanted to do something, but most days it feels like I can't do enough. I try to convince myself that it is still Mossie, just a different version and more bits gone with each visit. I didn't stay long. There was no glimmer of recognition. He was deep in the abyss.

And so, after the graveyard today I promised myself, I would pop over one last time, across to The Lough and that's what I did. And standing there I could hear us, solving the problems of the world, hear us ball-hopping, Seamus, Tom, Mossie, Paul, God rest him, falling in and Dan falling out. And I could see us on that bench, and I was not alone.

But most of all, I could feel them. Our conversations moving in time with the seasons, unrelenting, filled with the hope of spring as the daffodils bloomed around us, the energy of the hurlers by The Lough on long summer evenings, the contentment as autumn closed in and even with the gloom of short winter days.

Backbenchers. One of a kind. Creatures of habit. Me sitting front left, Mossie central, Dan front right, Seamus at his back, Tom keeping the peace and Paul…Paul back left. The backbenchers, quiet now with nothing more to say because it's all been said.

1972

A convent rooftop near Paris.
The Summer.

Helen Grace sat forward. She was hot, stifling hot. She looked to her side. Angela Delaney was fast asleep on her portion of the towel they were both sharing. Angela's blouse was lying in a heap where she had tossed it, while Helen's lay neatly folded. At Angela's feet, the football that never left her side. Helen could clearly make out two perfectly formed sunburn lines parallel to each side of Angela's lemon bra straps and the beads of sweat on the tips of her bra cups and underwire.

Helen checked herself and thanked God for her mother's side of the family. Helen's sallow skin was beginning to form a chestnut hue. She pushed her own bra forward for a peek of the virgin white skin of her own breasts. She smiled to herself. Would the rugby boys back in Callan find an erotic glimpse of white more alluring or incongruous? She remembered how Danny Walsh had felt cold to the touch and how she had reacted with a startled jump, frightening the living daylights out of the poor young fella into the bargain. She cupped herself. She felt warm. She turned her attention to Angela. Two newly formed red patches were clearly visible on her inner thighs. That wasn't good. She nudged Angela firmly.

"Are you awake?"

"I am now," Angela replied, sitting up groggily.

"You need to be careful," Helen advised. "You know what they say about sleeping in the sun. I had a friend one time, Mags Phelan, and she got burned to a crisp in Dunmore East. Blisters the size of golf balls she got." Helen shuddered at the memory of it.

"And you're telling me this, why? Because?" Angela's tone was filled with annoyance.

"In agony she was."

"And is that all you want to tell me? About Mags Phelan and her sunburn?" Angela continued, barely containing her irritation.

"I'm just saying."

"Good. I'll make note of it," Angela finished sarcastically, and she made to roll over on to her stomach, smoothing her portion of the towel as she did so. Helen adjusted herself also.

"Angela?"

"What now?"

"Nothing."

Angela rolled over on to her back once more, sat up and hugged her knees to her chest.

"Go on, I'm awake now," she said forlornly.

Helen pointed into the distance. "Those workers on that roof there. Do you think they can see us?"

Angela followed the trajectory of Helen's arm with curiosity and sure enough, there they were on an adjoining roof, three workmen with their backs hunched to the sun like mollusks.

"Do you want them to see us?" Angela asked mischievously.

"God no," Helen exclaimed, but Angela had already sprung to her feet and was waving her arms windmill-like in the direction of the men. "Hey over here!"

"Will you stop!" Helen said in panic.

Angela had her back to Helen now. She placed her index finger and middle finger between her lips and released a loud shrill whistle. "They can see us now alright," she laughed, turning back towards Helen.

"Jesus, Mary and Joseph," Helen gasped, ducking down sharply before scrambling to unfurl her blouse. She threw it around herself and began buttoning it up hectically. Angela remained unmoved.

"Do you think those French lads have ever seen a pair of fine strapping Irish girls before?" she guffawed, slapping her own hips. "And a good set of childbearing hips."

"Get down and behave yourself," Helen replied impatiently, but Angela took no notice of this reprimand and commenced to parade herself in a provocative manner. "And I have it on good authority," she proclaimed with certainty.

"What?"

Angela stopped and pirouetted towards Helen. "That I am well put together."

"Will you give over?"

"With a powerful behind."

"Just cover up or the nuns will have us excommunicated," Helen said briskly, throwing Angela her blouse. Angela caught the top and in one movement fired it back with interest. "'Tis up here they should be instead of praying all day and baking bread."

"Shh, they'll hear you."

"Shur, they won't be able to say anything anyway. Isn't that against their religion?"

"And for your information, it's Matins and Vespers. It's not just prayers."

"Do you not find it strange, though?" Angela probed. "All these women under one roof and not a peep out of them?"

Helen held out the blouse once more. "I don't, now will you please put that on."

"Yes mammy!" Angela snapped, taking the blouse grudgingly. She put it on slowly and began to button herself up painstakingly. When she had the blouse half done up, she began unbuttoning again with a flourish, humming *The Stripper* with gusto and dancing a series of exaggerated striptease actions.

"Jesus Angela!" Helen responded crossly.

"Alright, alright. We can't have the poor nuns getting overexcited. Bless us and save us," Angela conceded. She made a quick sign of the cross and finished tying up the garment efficiently. A sense of order descended once more and Helen was contented. "Mick was saying, if it wasn't for the nuns putting us up like this, we wouldn't have been able to play these games at all. There are some Irish nuns here who helped sort it."

"Imagine that, though. Getting away and ending up trapped here instead," Angela answered ruefully. "And he told me that the French crowd were scouting me last night. Introduced me to their coach after the game."

"Did he now?" Helen offered, barely concealing her surprise.

"Talked about me signing professional. Imagine that. Getting paid to play football."

Helen *knew* that was all Angela ever wanted and when she spoke of it, her face would light up in the anticipation of what that might be like for her. Helen also understood such a wrench would have consequences, not least for Bob and Kit, the grandparents who had raised Angela in north inner-city Dublin. That was a subject Angela spoke less of.

"And what did you say?" Helen asked composedly.

"I told him I'd think about it."

"And Bob and Kit?"

"They'll be grand," Angela dismissed. "He told me I was a little flyer."

"And who told you that?"

"Pierre, *toute vitesse,* to be exact."

Helen laughed at Angela's new-found command of the French language and raised her eyebrows quizzically. "Pierre?"

"Yes, their coach. Are you listening to me at all? Do you agree? That I'm a little flyer."

Helen made herself comfortable once more on the towel. "The first time I saw you."

"You don't think I'm too, stocky?" There was genuine concern in Angela's voice.

"I never thought about it."

"Mick says I have a low centre of gravity, perfect, he says for holding up play."

Helen scanned the opposite roof. The men seemed to have maintained working oblivious. "Mick has something to say to all the girls," she said vacantly.

Angela kneeled her left leg on to the towel and thrust her right thigh forward towards Helen.

"Feel that."

"What?"

"Go on," Angela encouraged.

Helen hesitantly took hold of Angela's thigh. It felt smooth and firm.

"Really press on it," Angela instructed.

Angela took Helen's hand in hers and guided her to press down on the flesh. Angela flexed her thigh and Helen could feel the muscular resistance.

"There," Angela said knowledgeably, "like tree trunks, he says. Well-built."

Helen removed her hands with a start. They had begun to get sticky, so she wiped them off her own thighs as she sat back down. "Well, he is not getting his dirty paws on my thighs! Yuch!!"

"He likes you," Angela said quickly as she stood again.

"Stop, you're giving me the creeps now!" Helen grimaced.

"Really?"

"God no. And you?"

"Mick thinks I can turn on a sixpence. Kept telling Pierre that after last night's game."

Angela made some space for herself. "Throw us that ball there. I'm bored now."

"For you to fall off the roof and break your two legs. I will not."

"Go on. Don't be such a killjoy. Mick says the ball should be an extension of your body. Control, control, control. Just lay it on for me there." Angela signaled for the ball, indicating where she wanted it exactly, but Helen plunged forward to scoop the ball into her chest. "You're not getting it!"

"Says who?" Angela responded sharply, and she made a quick darting motion to snatch the ball from Helen's grasp. The girls laughed instantaneously as they attempted to wrestle control of the football, and Helen was about to squirm her way free with the ball intact when Angela plunged her fingers under Helen's arm-pit and began tickling her. Helen fell back on to the towel, overcome with laughter. "Stop! Seriously, stop! I'm going to be sick!!"

Angela felt Helen's resistance relax, and she stood upright triumphantly, ball in hand. Helen sat up fixing herself on the towel. "You're some witch. That hurt!" she accused, rubbing herself fervently where Angela had grabbed her.

"I'm easy on the eye though," Angela batted back, a smile flashing across her face. She had liked that compliment when she had heard it first. She threw the ball up for herself. It was something all the team agreed on. When Angela and the ball were in full-flow she was indeed spell-binding. Helen shielded her eyes from the sun as Angela took two delicate first touches with her right foot, before shifting the ball effortlessly onto her left thigh. Her face was a study in concentration, arms low by her side, pony-tail bobbing gently behind her in rhythm with the movement of her body. She eased the ball back onto the side of her right foot before popping in naturally up onto her right knee. She then proceeded to interchange her touches from right to left foot, all the while with the ball under consummate control. Helen had seen her perform this movement many times at training, a gentle lofting of the ball up on to her right shoulder where she cushioned it before a final lean forward to secure the ball between her back and the nape of her neck.

But not today. Today, she allowed the ball drop from her right shoulder, and she pivoted at the final moment to smash the ball venomously skywards with her left foot. The ball sailed into the distance.

"Back of the net!" Angela shouted gleefully, and she punched the air in mock celebration.

"Cop on Angela! I'm serious." Helen's voice was filled with agitation.

"And so am I. The French girls play in an organised league, and the best ones can go on and play for their country."

But Helen was no longer paying attention as Angela laid out this potential football pathway for herself. Helen was staring intently into the distance, eyes fixed on the neighbouring roof.

"Jesus, Angela, you really have gone and done it this time!"

*

He was young, tall, and a shock of black unkempt curly shoulder-length hair partially obscured his deep brown eyes. His striped t-shirt was sweat-stained from the work and his work pants was mottled with timber shavings and had an array of pockets from which protruded various tool handles at differing angles. They looked inviting, waiting to be touched. Neither girl had seen teeth so even, teeth that gleamed the way his seemed to, but it was his right hand that drew all their attention. There, balanced perfectly on the upturned palm, was Angela's football.

"Girls. I think this is yours, no?" he held the ball out for closer inspection, his lilting French accent peppering the air.

"Thanks. Got it in one." Angela's response was curt. With that, he lofted the ball gently to her. "You girls are enjoying the good weather?"

"We are, and you?" Angela nodded, securing the ball under her arm.

"Working, fixing the leak."

Angela turned to Helen. "Do hear that, Helen? The nuns have a leak."

"On the roof," he added.

"The best place to have one," Angela smiled.

"Pardon?" His face remained expressionless.

"Ah 'tis nothing. We are only messing with you, fella." Angela's face softened.

He took the opportunity to step closer. "You are the Irish girls, yes? The footballers staying at La Carthusian."

Angela took the lead. "That's us in the flesh. Isn't that right Helen. Gosh my apologies. We haven't even introduced ourselves. You must think we are a right shower." She also stepped forward and, wiping her right on her shorts, offered it to him. "I'm Angela, Angela Grace."

"Pleased to meet you Angela, and I'm Luc, Luc Dugarry," he replied, taking her hand and shaking it politely.

Helen stepped to Angela's side and gave a quick demure wave. "Hi, and I'm Helen."

"Hello Angela and Helen," he chimed, taking a step back once more, his voice warm.

"And do you play football yourself?" Helen asked, folding her arms across her chest, self-consciously.

"A little." Luc ran a hand through his tousled hair.

"And what else do you do when you are not fixing roofs?" Angela added.

"I study at the Sorbonne in Paris. My first year. I wish to become a teacher and travel also."

"Wow." Helen's eyes shone with excitement, and Angela threw her a look. "And have you been to Ireland yet?" Angela asked calmly.

"Not yet. I wish to go some day. I spent two months in London last summer to improve my English, and this summer I fix roofs." Luc tossed his head back resignedly.

"And when you do come, we will show you round," Helen interjected enthusiastically.

"I would like that."

"No bother," Helen gestured, looking him directly in the eye.

"And what do you girls do when you are not playing football on the roof?"

Angela raised her hand before Helen could answer. "Me? I work in a factory in Dublin. It's not what I want, but it pays well. Most of the team are there and the manager," she offered up dolefully. Angela's take on her own situation was not a new revelation for Helen, and she stepped beyond her, within touching distance of Luc now. "But what Angela really wants to do is play football for a living in France. Don't you Angela?"

"Amazing. You must be truly excellent." A smile spread across Luc's face.

"Angela can turn on a sixpence."

Luc's gaze was totally set on Helen now. "And what about you? *Pouvez-vous allumer un six pence?*"

"Sorry?" Helen looked perplexed.

Luc laughed. "And now I'm...how do you say? Only messing with you." He patted Helen playfully. "And what would you like to do?"

Helen felt herself blushing. "I would also like to go to college," she began thoughtfully, before pausing, "but it's...I don't live in Dublin. I from down the country, in the south," she finished.

"Not a factory girl." Luc continued to examine her intently.

"No, Mick the manager saw me paying one weekend in Kilkenny and asked me to come on this trip. I couldn't say no. A chance to play, travel and see Paris."

"And the nuns look after you well, yes?"

Both Helen and Angela nodded their approval in unison. "Of course. Couldn't be better."

"But maybe they are not so happy to see me here a man on this roof, the roof without a leak," he smiled once more.

"We won't spill the beans, if you don't," Angela suggested conspiratorially.

"And now my boss, he wonders where I am, and I must say *Au Revoir*."

Angela tapped the football. "And thanks for bringing our ball back.

Luc turned to leave, but as he did, he stopped himself. "You are both welcome. And will I see you again?"

Neither girl could have sworn to it, but it appeared this request might just have been directed at Helen.

"You can watch us play Saturday if you like," she answered eagerly.

"I would like that. And before Saturday?"

"You can if you like," Helen replied indifferently

"*Jusqu'a la prochaine fois,*" Luc turned and made his way across the roof. The girl's gazes followed him. They watched him as stepped over the ledge onto the adjacent roof and rejoined his work colleagues.

"What do you think?" Helen asked giddily.

"Not my cup of tea," Angela answered dully. She tossed Helen the ball. "And you?"

"A bit, like yourself, Angela girl," Helen joked, "easy on the eye!"

*

Sr. Monica loved the solitude of the roof at this time of the day. She went there every evening to pray, the faint singing of the sisters from the chapel her only back-drop. The day had been excessively hot, and now the refreshing higher air was a pleasant relief for her. She enjoyed this time to herself, but to-night was different. She felt a presence. She was not alone. She looked over her the shoulder just in time to see the young girl stop in her tracks. She was boyish in appearance, a purple band keeping her short hair off her forehead, but her sallow skin was flawless, t-shirt, shorts and plimsolls. As their eyes met, there was a look of complete mortifi-cation on the young girl's face.

"O God, I didn't realise, I'm so sorry, sister," the girl spluttered.

"Don't be."

"I didn't mean to intrude, I'll let you be." She sound-ed like she wished the ground would swallow her up.

"No don't go," Sr. Monica said reassuringly.

The young girl seemed wracked with indecision. "I should. The others will be wondering where I've got to," she answered apologetically.

"And are you enjoying your stay?"

"Brilliant."

"Good," Sr. Monica said encouragingly. "And the football?"

The question seemed to settle her.

"We drew a game and play again Saturday." She made another attempt to back away. "I'm really sorry for bothering you."

Sr. Monica beckoned the girl to join her. "No, please stay, sit awhile."

As the girl crossed timidly and sat beside her, they both took a moment to saviour the evening.

"It is nice here," the girl said thoughtfully.

"I think so. I like to come here during recreation hour. It is peaceful. I can think. Talk to God."

"I really should leave," the girl suggested awkwardly.

Sr. Monica shook her head gently. "Don't be silly. Please stay a while longer. It's not often we have visitors and from home too."

"I will so sister. I'm Helen, Helen Grace," she offered her hand.

"And call me Monica, please." The handshake was brief.

"Monica," Helen repeated the name to herself. "It is peaceful here, peaceful but…" she hesitated.

"Go on, child," Sr. Monica encouraged.

"I don't think I could live like this."

"And I'll let you in on a little secret, Helen. That was me once. The not knowing I could do it."

"And what changed?"

"Now I know I can."

Helen thought for a moment. "How can you be so sure?"

"Nobody is ever fully sure, are they? So, every evening I come up here and talk to God. He listens."

"And your family and friends?"

"The sisters are my family now. And yourself? Where are you from?"

"Bennettsbridge."

"Lovely. I grew up in Ross, Rosscarberry. My parents have a pub there, O'Donnell's. My brother runs it now. I spent many happy summers there.

"And did you ever play a bit of ball?"

"No. It was frowned upon."

Helen watched her closely as she spoke. In comparison to how she was coping to herself with the muggy heat, Sr. Monica seemed cool and serene. It was difficult to make out her features with the veil and white headdress which framed her head and seemed to constrain her upper body, but there wasn't a stray hair in sight. Although Helen could make out the beginning of some faint lines around her eyes and the corner of her mouth, she thought it impossible to put an age on her. The one unquestionable was that an ease had descended between them and Helen felt completely comfortable as Sr. Monica opened up even further, sharing with her how she had made a choice in her life, wanted God in her life and never wanted to forget his presence, leaving Ireland when she was "ready, ready to learn and ready to help others." Helen listened attentively, barely interrupting as Sr. Monica detailed that it hadn't all been plain sailing and that she had relied on the power of prayer to make the right choices in the face of strident opposition from her father, who had tried to get her to "see sense."

"You make it sound so easy," Helen mused.

"God lifts our prayers and makes them useful."

"I want to go to college in Dublin," Helen blurted in response and immediately felt embarrassed.

"Good for you," Sr. Monica nodded in agreement.

"I want a life. To meet new people, make new friends, meet boys, you know what I mean," Helen attempted to explain further.

"I do."

"And did you ever want that?" Helen asked shyly.

"My life is busy thanking God, just in different ways."

"I want to be free to do what I want to do," Helen said with more conviction.

"And can you not do that at home?"

"No sister."

Sr. Monica grimaced briefly. "Monica, please, or Linda if you like. I haven't been called that for a while."

Helen considered what Sr. Monica had just told her, considered it as a sharing of sorts, an intimacy.

"Linda, why that's a beautiful name," she concluded.

"Sometimes I miss it. Monica is my Carthusian name. Linda O'Donnell, that's what the Ross crowd would know me by. Paddy and Bernie's young one who ran away to be a nun." She gave a hearty laugh.

"Ran off?"

"Stories get legs. They couldn't understand why I didn't want an eligible young farmer."

Sitting beside each other as they were, Helen could not help but notice Sr. Monica's porcelain-like skin, piercing blue eyes, angular cheekbones and jaw line.

Her fingers were long and delicate and also appeared bloodless. In her mind's eye, Helen tried to marry this version of Sr. Monica with another image of her as a West Cork farmer's wife, Fair Isle jumper, oilskins tucked inside her wellies, yard brush in hand, cleaning down an outhouse steaming in hot cow shite.

"And was there ever a boy, an eligible farmer?" she asked brightly.

"Maybe one." Sr. Monica's tone was flat.

"And what became of him?"

"It was nothing. Short-lived. We kissed a few times. Held hands once."

"That doesn't sound like nothing to me," Helen said with certainty.

"It was to me."

"And did you ever?" Helen was shocked by the personal nature of her own question and tried to disguise that.

"Lord no. Nothing like that. It never made me feel I wanted to act."

"And him?"

"Told me one time that I made him feel wanted and that he wanted me."

Sr. Monica scanned the horizon and Helen tried to make sense of what Linda O'Donnell from Roscarrberry was laying out before her so coldly. She tried to reconcile it with her own absolute desire to want to be with a boy one day. As she listened further it became even more difficult for her to fathom, Sr. Monica's complete conviction that such a marriage was not how she wanted to be seen in the world and her unyielding belief that there was more purpose to her life here in France, having given herself to God and his mission for her. As their conversation unfolded, Helen had no doubt that Sr. Monica truly believed that she also had a freedom to do what she wanted in her life.

"And the eligible farmer?"

"I joined La Carthusian and never saw him again."

"And did you tell him how you felt?"

"No."

"I think you should have."

"And why do you think that?"

"For his sake, if nothing else."

"I didn't feel the need."

"And your father?"

"We lost contact."

That, above all everything else, Helen struggled with the most. She could never envisage that. Her mother had died young, and her father had never taken on another woman to replace her. It had always been just him and Helen, eking out a life in that small cottage at the edge of the village. Helen knew the locals talked of her mother's death as a shocking blow, but her passing was part of who herself and her father had become, and now there was the guilt of wanting to go to college and the worry of how he might cope alone. She had mentioned it to him in passing, but they had never sat down and fleshed out the detail of what Helen's actual moving to Dublin might entail, or the costs involved in such a move. She knew deep down that ultimately he would never stand in her way, and he would offer assurances that it would be what her mother would have wanted and that he himself would be bursting with pride for her. None of this eased her feelings of disquiet.

"I worry," Helen confided.

"Worries are only normal," Sr. Monica replied evenly. "God can help you with those."

"God is your answer to everything," Helen exclaimed in frustration and immediately regretted the outburst. "I'm sorry, Monica. I've no right to say that. You nuns have been nothing but good to us since we arrived," she corrected.

"Putting your trust in God for guidance isn't easy. There is a risk in really letting go."

"But turning your back on your family and friends," Helen shrugged in confusion, "it's not natural."

"It's not the first time that's been said," Sr. Monica answered cryptically.

"Your father?"

"Yes."

"Maybe if he could come out and visit, see for himself," Helen suggested.

"Maybe, but it's not encouraged."

"And the boy?"

"What about him?"

"Maybe you could help him to move on. Maybe that's all they both need, a gentle nudge."

"I'll keep that in mind if you do one thing for me."

"What's that sister?"

"To live the life God gave you."

"I'll try."

"Will you pray with me so, for both?"

Sr. Monica offered Helen her hand and she took it without compulsion. Sr. Monica then leaned forward in silent prayer, and Helen followed her lead. At that moment, it felt to Helen like the most natural thing in the world. In the distance, the chapel was quiet.

*

From her vantage point on the roof's balcony, she surveyed the chapel below. Angela was standing with her back to Helen, hands placed squarely on the ledge, allowing the cooler morning air caress her face. She could barely contain her bafflement.

"And that's all she had to say for herself, this Irish nun. That it was all God's plan."

"Yes," Helen answered sheepishly.

Angela turned to face Helen, resting her back against the ledge. "That's bonkers," she chuckled.

"She made it sound like the right thing to do for her."

"Praying and baking bread all day. How can that make sense?" Angela was unrelenting.

"You didn't meet her," Helen argued defiantly.

"Can we just talk about something else so?" Angela turned to face the chapel once more.

Helen did want to talk about something else, ever since the subject had been broached the previous day. She was bothered. She knew that Angela would never do anything intentionally to hurt Bob and Kit. Angela idolised her grandparents. They had after all taken her in and reared her as their own when Angela's father had gone to England, and it had all gotten too much for mother, but Helen was fearful that all this heady talk of a contract in France would cloud Angela's judgement. Angela needed to stay grounded, and this was Helen's opportunity.

"Professional football. How does that even work?"

"I'll know more tomorrow. Mick is bringing me to meet Pierre again."

"And when were you going to tell me this?" Helen asked accusingly.

"Amn't I telling you now," Angela cracked, turning angrily.

"And what is this meeting about?"

"Another chat."

"Just a chat?"

Angela threw her arms out in frustration. "Jesus, I don't know, Helen. If Saturday goes well. Who knows."

"And when are you going to tell them at home about this?"

"Soon." Angela turned away, disgruntled.

Helen left it lie. She had to tread carefully. Football was the only oulet that meant something to Angela. It brought her alive, the one aspect of her life where she could hold her head up and say look at me. Helen didn't want to push her away. She crossed to join her and placed one hand gently on her back. "So, what's the plan?"

"You really are a great person, Helen," Angela sighed, leaning her head into Helen's shoulder.

"What do you mean?"

Angela turned her head and fixed her eyes on Helen. "There's no backdoors with you. You tell it as it is."

"Thanks."

Helen could feel her throat tighten. She thought of her father and how growing up he had instilled that trait in her, and she remembered the night her mother died and how as a six-year-old girl she was brought to her mother's bedside. Her mother had taken Helen's hand in hers, Helen never forgetting the weakness of the grip, and looking up from her deathbed her mother had whispered, "be an honest girl now for your mammy and pray for me." Her mother had held Helen's hand then briefly before allowing it to slip away.

Helen could feel herself welling up.

"Jesus, come here to me. I'm sorry for upsetting you." Angela embraced Helen.

"Look at the state of me." Helen's voice was a mixture of laughter and tears as she fought to compose herself.

"Here, let me." Angela took a hanky from her pocket and dabbed Helen's tears. The girls were looking at each other now, their faces within touching distance.

"And now you have started me off," Angela sobbed.

"What are we like, the pair of us," Helen laughed, holding back fresh tears.

"No, you are spot on, Helen. I need to do right. Be true to myself," Angela sniffled.

Helen threw her arms around Angela in a comforting hug. "It will work out fine, you'll see." before releasing her and leaving her hands on her shoulders.

"Let me tidy you up now," she offered, taking the hanky off Angela and wiping her face clean.

"How do I look?" Angela asked.

Helen took a step back to take stock. "You look, beautiful again."

"I just feel…I don't know what I feel," Angela faltered.

Helen placed the palm of her hand on Angela's breastbone. "Your heart is racing."

"It is, isn't it. It's so stupid." Angela cast her eyes down.

Helen took Angela's hand in her own and placed it on Angela's beating heart, holding it there soothingly.

"Feel that," Helen said quietly.

"I know, silly."

"Listen. It's so quiet up here," Helen murmured. "Can you feel it?"

With that, Angela leaned her forward and kissed Helen on the lips.

*

Helen needed to clear her head. She needed this time away from football, from her teammates, Mick and away from…

"And where is Angela today?" Luc asked casually. He was pacing the roof before her, taking in the views.

"She had to meet someone," Helen answered indifferently.

"Sounds, how do you say? Very mysterious."

"Well, I'm sure it's not."

"And Angela did not ask you to come with her to meet someone?"

"I had no interest."

"And Angela she was happy, no, to go alone."

"Why do you keep asking me about Angela?" Helen fired irritably. "I don't really care what she thinks. I told you I had no interest."

Luc stopped and made a gesture of surrender. "My pardon. Maybe you also want to be alone today." And he turned to leave.

"No, wait. Don't go. I'm sorry for snapping like that," Helen answered guiltily. "I'd like you to stay, if you want to, that is."

"No, it is my fault. I should not poke my nose in other people's business."

"And I shouldn't be such a bitch," Helen acknowledged.

Luc crouched over her and signaled for permission to sit alongside. "May I?"

"Of course."

"*Je ne pense pas tu es un chienne,*" Luc said lightly as he took his place beside her.

"And what does that mean?" Helen frowned.

"It means I like you. Not a bitch. Ok."

The beginnings of a faint smile crept across Helen's face. "I can be sometimes," she admitted.

"And today is one of those days?"

"It might be," Helen added candidly. "You see myself and Angela, we had a…misunderstanding."

"Shh," Luc stopped her elaborating. "No more talk about Angela. We agreed."

"We did," Helen laughed, throwing her head back. "And that sun. It looks like you could pluck it right out of the sky."

"Lie back," Luc suggested eagerly.

"What?" Helen's face was awry with confusion.

"Trust me. Just lie back. We can do this together."

Helen reluctantly did as Luc asked and, beside her, he was doing likewise.

"Now reach out as far as you can and block the sun with the palm of your right hand."

Helen giggled, tilted her head towards him and followed his lead.

"Hold your palm there and relax. Very slowly now make a fist. Be careful, *peu a peu.* Close your eyes and when I count to three sit up gradually. "Don't drop it. Eyes closed, *un, deux, trois."*

"What are we like!" Helen joked, doing as he did.

They were both sitting upright now with their right hands clenched.

"Open your eyes, but don't drop it." Luc turned to face Helen and looked at her deeply. "I will give you mine first and keep it safely, yes. Show me your other hand."

Helen held out her left hand and as she did Luc cupped his right hand over it. "And now you nice and gentle."

Helen followed suit, her right hand to his left. As she did, their eyes met once more. His face was a blend of manliness and gentility. She felt lightheaded, her pulse quickening and her colour rising.

"We have exchanged a special gift now," Luc said earnestly. "The gift of sunlight. Keep it safe, where you can visit it anytime." He placed his left hand over his own heart. Helen smiled and touched the side of her head. "I will." Her eyes were sparkling.

"And now you smile, lovely again."

"So, maybe I won't be a bitch today after all."

"And to-night we will reach for the stars."

"Tonight?"

They drew back from each other.

"Yes, a proper date," Luc nodded. "Me and you. It is ok, yes."

"Yes, I would like that," Helen smiled, reaching out and resting her hand on his.

*

Angela was alone. She was absolutely livid with herself. The one true friend she could confide in, share with. How could she have gotten the signals so badly wrong? All day, when she had thought about it, she had felt nauseated. And now there she was crossing the roof purposefully. Angela's face froze.

"I was wondering where I'd find you."

"I needed some place to think," Angela said broodingly.

"Can I stay?" Helen asked.

"If you want to." Angela looked away.

Helen sat beside her. "What do you think?" she asked willfully.

"Honestly," Angela swallowed and looked at Helen softly in the eyes, "I don't know. Are we ok, the two of us, after...yesterday?" Angela lowered her head.

"I'm here, aren't I?"

"Still friends so." There was a strain in Angela's voice, and she shifted uneasily where she sat. A smile widened across Helen's face.

"Of course we are you, silly goat. Now, to be fair, I didn't know you fancied me!" Helen said breezily.

"I don't," Angela exhaled.

Helen placed her arm around Angela's shoulder. "And as much as I love you…"

"Not like that," Angela finished the sentence for her.

"No."

"It's something between us now," Angela suggested circumspectly.

"And that's where it will stay."

Angela allowed herself to relax. Helen's assuagement confirmed for her what she always believed to be true that Helen was indeed a good decent person, a fearless person and as they sat side by side in comfortable silence Angela took the opportunity to divulge to this good friend that, she was finally coming to the realisation that she couldn't live this life of secrecy anymore, but that she needed more time to "work it through" and for once in her life "try and put herself first".

Growing up Angela had never felt any attraction for the boys in her neighbourhood. She had used them as a means to an end to improve herself as a football player, but her deeper desires she had kept suppressed. As a teenager, that had been difficult for her, the confusion. At first, it had appeared easier to live the lie, but that had meant that the world away from the football pitch had been a troubled and lonely place for her. These were the feelings she felt she could never reveal to Bob or Kit, and that added to the melancholy of her young adulthood. There had been one brief, fleeting period of respite during her final year at school, a furtive relationship with an older girl. Angela had believed this girl when she had said nice things to her, believed she was telling the truth. And then the crushing blow when she told Angela that for her, it was just a bit of "messing around", "experimenting."

Angela looked at Helen. Her eyes were warm and filled with understanding.

"What happened after that?" Helen asked kindly.

"We stopped being close."

"Well, we won't," she said definitively.

"Thanks Helen. That means a lot to me."

Helen leaned towards Angela. "Now come on, tell me how that meeting went this morning?"

"They want me to sign, after the game tomorrow. What I always wanted," Angela answered drearily.

Helen clapped her hands with delight and thrust herself forward. "That's brilliant news. You see things are looking up."

"Then why do I feel so miserable?"

"Because we are Irish. We are born that way." Helen jumped to her feet. "Let's celebrate." She crouched and began to haul Angela upright also.

"It's not straightforward," Angela said reticently, straightening herself. "They want me to start immediately."

"And what did you say?"

"That I'd think about it."

"And have you?"

"All my life."

"Well then."

Angela shrugged and walked to the roof edge.

"Whatever makes you less miserable," Helen cautioned.

"And back home?" Angela asked quietly, scanning the horizon.

"Talk it all through with them. Tell them everything. How you feel?"

Angela turned to face Helen. Her face was filled with doubt. "Everything?"

"Yes."

"No, Helen, I couldn't face that."

*

Some evenings, prayers came easier than others for Sr. Monica. She had felt a deep unquiet all day, and her acquired understanding of how God liked to test her from time to time did little to quell her apprehension. She knew that one passed these tests by being patient, by listening and by waiting. She had immersed herself in the Carthusian teachings, the importance of faith and the opening of one's mind and heart to allow the sign to come. She truly believed that the simplest thing in the world was to allow Jesus into her life, to make time for it, to follow it, believe it, and finally to put your life in the hands of the greater power. She had followed La Carthusian to a fault, yet tonight she could not shake the nagging doubts. Where once she thrived in its solitude, now she was glad to see the young vibrant Irish girl enter the roof space once more. She reminded her of herself in a different lifetime. Was this God's ultimate test for her?

Can I ask you something?" Helen enquired tentatively.

"Of course."

"A personal question."

"Go ahead."

Helen took a slow breath. "Do you miss her?"

"Who?" Sr. Monica looked puzzled.

"Linda."

"I have no regrets, if that's what you mean," Sr. Monica said calmly.

"None." Helen's tone was filled with surprise.

"Linda had no direction in her life."

Helen took a moment. She needed to get her head around Sr. Monica referring to herself in the third person. It was disconcerting for her. "But don't you ever wonder about that life?"

"Today, all day, I have been pre-occupied. Something you said yesterday," Sr. Monica answered thoughtfully.

"It wouldn't be the first time I put my foot in it."

"You asked me had I ever played football. That was something we would never even dream of doing, been allowed to even contemplate and now, this life, this is my choice. I don't expect you to understand that. Not in a weekend."

Helen was watching Sr. Monica's studiously, but her face was betraying no emotion.

"And then it got me thinking about Ross," she continued, "what was expected of me, Linda. I don't miss that. And I have thought about my father today, for the first time in a long time."

"Have you made a decision?" Helen interrupted.

"No."

"And the boy?"

"John, and he was just a boy. So, I have been thinking about this, and it's been troubling me all day that maybe I do miss her, but not her life. Can you understand that?"

"It makes perfect sense to me," Helen agreed.

"That I don't want to lose that part of myself."

"That's not a sin, is it? To want to be yourself."

Sr. Monica allowed herself a faint knowing smile. "The sisters say doubts are sent to challenge us. To make us stronger."

"Your father, this boy John, they are part of who you are not doubts."

"What are you saying?"

"Not to forget that."

"Sometimes Linda can make life difficult for me," Sr. Monica admitted, joining her hands.

"Maybe, she just needs to stop running."

"I hope you get what you want, Helen, you truly deserve it." Sr. Monica then raised her right arm and offered Helen a blessing.

"I'll find a way. I always do."

"Promise me that."

"If you do one thing for me."

"If I can."

"Those days Linda O'Donnell from Rosscarberry is making life hard for you, you need to make peace with her. Will you do that for me?"

"Deal."

They exchanged a brief hug and as Sr. Monica watched Helen leave, she felt comforted. This young Irish girl had spoken openly, honestly and bravely. Sr. Monica moved to the balconies edge and looked out at the reddening night sky. She knew it was thought inappropriate in the public areas, but she couldn't resist the overwhelming urge. She slowly and meticulously unclipped her veil, removed her *bandeau* and shook her hair free and for one daring moment she was Linda O'-Donnell once more.

*

Helen and Luc were both lying facing skywards, hand in hand. Helen had never seen anything quite like this indigo sky mottled in every direction as far as the eye could see with clear stars. Earlier in the evening had been equally impressive. While the team had gone to an Irish bar in the *18th Arrondissement* to celebrate their victory, Luc had taken Helen to see Paris in all its glory. The sights, sounds, and smells of the city had fascinated her, and she felt practically drunk from the exuberance of it all.

What had been most striking had been the riot of colour at each site: The Arc de Triomphe, The Eiffel Tower, a far cry from the staid black and white images she had been exposed to in her school books. Before her very eyes, these monochrome images of her mind's eye exploded into living, breathing places. The sounds of the city equally enthralled her, the honking of car horns, the chatter of French accents, and she had stepped endearingly around the footpath grilles that allowed blasts of hot air to escape as the metro's trundled below.

The conversation had flowed naturally between them, and Luc had told her of his upbringing in Crisenoy, a small village outside of Paris. He spoke openly about how in the beginning he had found life at the Sorbonne difficult. He had been torn by loneliness when he arrived first, conflicted by the pull of Crisenoy, the place his ambition was always to leave. Initially, all he wanted to do was go back there, but he explained how eventually these feelings passed and now being away from home and loved ones felt perfectly normal.

Helen felt comfortable in his presence and shared her worries about leaving her father to pursue her own dreams. Luc reassured her that it was alright to feel these emotions, but that everybodys life must change. "You will love it," he had enthused. "And your father will be happy because you are happy." Helen hadn't wanted the evening to end, and she knew she would remember it for the rest of her life, remember this night, no matter how many times she would return to Paris, and she was determined to return one day. And so, they had found themselves back on the roof where they first met only a few days previously.

"What are you thinking?" Helen asked shyly.

"That this is very beautiful, and you?"

"That we are very small."

"*Petite.*"

"Two tiny dots."

"*Deux petits points.*"

"And the stars?"

"*L'etoiles.*"

"Doesn't the whole world seem, very...fragile," Helen pondered.

"The Gods are very happy tonight. The stars create life. What is within the stars is life itself."

Helen gave a little laugh, sat forward and released his hand. "Do you believe that?"

"Of course."

"What do you see in the stars?" she asked, looking across at him with curiosity.

"That your eyes are..." Luc's voice faded.

"What about them?"

"They are...Can I kiss you?"

"You don't need to ask."

"But the kiss is the most precious of all. It must never be stolen," Luc said sitting up beside her.

"Our manger tried to kiss me once."

"What happened?"

"I brushed him off."

Luc leaned towards her and his fingers brushed her cheek as he pushed her hair back from her face. He cupped his hands and eased her towards him. "Do you want to brush me off?" he smiled gently. Their lips were touching softly now.

"No," Helen sighed in breathless anticipation as she felt the warmth of his touch under her blouse.

*

The two girls had come to squeeze as much time out of the glorious weather as they could muster. Helen had her arms out by her side to prop herself up. Her eyes were closed, and she had her face pointing directly in the line of fire of the sun. She could feel her forehead, face and breastbone getting hot, but she didn't care anymore. Beside her, Angela was engrossed in the morning newspaper Mick had brought back from the village. She was using her thumb and index finger to snap through the pages mercilessly.

"It was everything I thought it would be," Helen said confidentially, but the only reply was the sound of page slapping on page.

"Are you even listening to me?" Helen turned to Angela, her voice filled with aggravation.

"I am. It was everything you thought it would be," Angela recited back without lifting her head.

"What?" Helen challenged.

"Paris," Angela answered, finally looking up and raising her eyebrows.

"My point exactly. You haven't been listening to a word I've been saying. Me and Luc."

"You need to be careful with those French lads. They only want one thing from a girl," Angela warned.

"And Mick?"

"Mick has done a lot for me."

"He is still a slim-ball though," Helen retorted.

"He is," Angela agreed. "Now take a look at that." Angela smoothed the newspaper out across her thighs with the palm of her hand.

"What am I looking for?"

"See do you recognise anyone," Angela replied, brandishing a smile.

Helen didn't need to look twice. There she was in black and white, in all her glory, Angela. She was balancing balletically on her right foot, body arched in unison and her face a study in concentration. She was about to shift the ball beyond her French opponent with her left foot and cut back inside. The French girl had the pained look of defeat on her face, the dawning realisation that in an instant Angela would be gone, leaving her in her wake. She was flailing hopelessly, trying to catch hold of Angela's right cuff.

"Sweetest Jesus!" Helen proclaimed. "That's you and that's the goal."

"I'm famous," Angela smiled proudly.

Helen peered closely at the caption beneath the photograph:

Cette femme est dangereuse.

"They think I'm dangerous!" Angela emphasised wildly.

"Brilliant!" Helen threw her head back freely, clapping her hands.

Angela began to fold the newspaper, and she handed it to Helen. "Will you show it to Bob and Kit when you get back?"

"And can't you do that? Helen asked, holding the paper out from her body awkwardly.

"I wish you had come back to the bar with us, Helen. We had a glass of champagne to celebrate, and they are going to pay me twenty French pounds a week." Angela's eyes were sparkling with exhilaration. "And I need you to do that massive favour for me."

"This." Helen gave the paper a slight wave and scrunched her face up in unsureness.

"Yes."

"I don't understand." Helen sounded bewildered.

"They want me to start straightaway. Three games in Italy next month, pre-season."

At first, Helen's bafflement deepened, the blur of how Angela did not intend travelling home to Ireland in the morning instead embarking on her new life for herself and imposing on Helen to smooth this decision over with her grandparents, just to tide Angela over until things settled down, but Helen quickly gathered herself.

"Not a hope," Helen said staunchly.

"But I can make a life here, the life I want to live, the way I want to live it."

"I can't do this," Helen pleaded, her voice shaking with every word.

"I promise I will explain everything the first chance I get."

"Everything."

"Yes."

"Promise."

Angela blessed herself resolutely. "I give you, my word. I can get home for Christmas."

"Christmas," Helen enunciated.

"I wouldn't ask you, but I need someone I can trust."

Helen made to hand back the newspaper to Angela.

"Can you do this for me, please? I'm begging you."

"You better look after yourself," Helen said, taking the newspaper back and setting it down beside her, "and score some goals."

The girls exchanged a long hug and in the intensity of the moment didn't realise they were no longer without company.

"*Bonjour mes demoiselles.*" Luc's greeting was in keeping with the brightness of the day. "I came to say *au revoir* to you both, and I brought a gift for everyone." He was carrying a brown bag close to his chest.

Angela shifted to one side and made room for Luc to sit between them. "Squeeze in there, so nice and cosy!"

Luc sat between them, placing the bag between his legs.

"And Angela has news Luc. She is staying here in France to play football."

"*Fantastique!* We can drink to that." Luc took three bottles from the bag."

"What's that?" Helen asked.

"*Coca,*" Luca replied, handing her one of the bottles. She took the bottle gingerly and ran her hand over its curved shape. "I've never seen it."

"*Boisson non alcoolise,* a soda," Luc explained as he handed Angela a bottle. "Do you think you will spend many years in professional football, Angela?"

"I hope so," Angela said as both herself and Helen held their bottles up for closer inspection.

"Please allow me," Luc said, and he produced a *Swiss Army Knife* from his pocket and systematically began opening the bottles with the corkscrew, first Helen, then Angela and finally himself. He raised his own bottle theatrically, then, *"Sante!* to Angela, her football, *l'avenir."* They clinked their glasses then before drinking in silence.

Angela was the first to speak. "Pretty good." She then held the bottle up towards the sun again.

"Helen? *C'est delicieux,* tastes good, no," Luc asked approvingly.

"Sweet."

"Bon gout."

"That's it...bon gout," Helen repeated.

*

Helen had never gone that far with a boy before, and she was glad it had been with Luc. She had nearly been overwhelmed as her body convulsed under the lightness of his touch down there before she took his arousal in her hand. At first, he had placed his hand over hers and guided the slow rhythmic movement before trusting her to finish. She was pleased that he had surrendered himself in this way to the sensitivity of her touch and at the moment of climax she also had felt a frisson of energy course through her own body as his body shuddered, and his face contorted in ecstasy. And then she held him tenderly as he emptied himself fully and his breathing became shallower. At that moment, she was taken by the heat of him, and then he slumped into her arms. It had been an awakening for her, and she knew that on returning home, the feeble fumbling of the lads down the rugby club would never be enough to satisfy her. She had basked in the intimate warmth of it all day, but now the inevitability of a parting hung between them.

"Will I see you again?" Luc asked Helen, fixing her an inquisitive look.

"When you come to Ireland."

"And that makes me a little sad."

"You must go back to college and I must…I know what I want now. Anything else wouldn't be fair on either of us."

"I want to show you something," Luc said, taking Helen by the hand.

"Where?"

"Something special." Luc led Helen across the roof to the balcony ledge and pointed into the middle-distance. "Look, just there," he advised, shifting Helen's body lightly in the direction he was pointing. "There, through the trees…*la tourelle, a gauche.* That roof, *la rose,* the pink one."

There in the glare of the sun, Helen could make out a pink domed building, its green roof tiles glistening in the sun.

"Yes, I can see it."

"*Chateau Marianne,*" Luc said dramatically.

"It is very beautiful."

"*La famille Duplessis* had it built for their daughter Marianne and her lover Jean when he left to fight the British at Gibraltar. It was a famous battle." Luc's voice was soft, controlled.

"The Brits are always fighting someone." Helen screwed her face up in disgust.

"Built as a symbol of their love to each other." Luc placed his left arm on Helen's shoulder and leaned across her with his right hand pointing forward. "If you look closely, you can see the J and M, the initials of the two lovers on that roof there." Helen took her guide from Luc and strained her eyes. "Yes, I can make that out."

Luc stooped forward slightly. "And now look below, the two hands joined as a symbol of fidelity."

"I see them."

"And now I will make a memory for both of us that will not evaporate." Luc straightened himself. The Swiss Army Knife was out again, and he began etching on the wooden handrail.

"What are you doing? Helen recoiled in shock.

"Wait and see." Luc was concentrating fully on the handrail, moving along it slowly working the knife in his right hand, and clearing away the shavings into the summer air with his left. "In France we say nothing can separate those who love each other, not even time."

"Jesus, stop! The nuns will blow a gasket!"

Luc continued, head bent, finished the carving and wiped it with his sleeve before standing back proudly. "And now nothing can come between us, look." He closed the knife shut and returned it to his pocket. Helen stepped forward and ran her finger along the fresh carving:

L & H

Trentiemme du Julliet, dix-neuf soixante-douze

She turned her head to Luc. "And what happened the two lovers?"

"He never returned. Marianne lived a long life with many husbands, but Jean was always her true love."

Helen read the inscription aloud. "L and H, July thirtieth, nineteen seventy-two."

"You're last day in France."

"No doom and gloom, not today. Say something in French, something nice, something we will remember."

*"Aujourd'hui est le premier jour du reste de nos vies...*I said..."

But before Luc could explain, Helen had placed her hand on his lips. "Shh stop. I don't need to know. Just hold me one more time like before."

*

Sr. Monica was exactly where Helen had expected to find her. Helen wanted to thank her for the hospitality, but also needed to tell her that her mind was settled, and she was determined to set the train in motion on arrival back in Bennettsbridge. She would sit her father down and have a proper heart-to-heart. They could work something out.

"Our prayers were answered so," Sr. Monica smiled benignly.

"They were weren't they."

"And I learned some things about myself," she confided.

"What kind of things?" Helen looked surprised.

"That I wasn't happy and a bit lost. I listened to what you had to say," Sr. Monica said with a half-smile.

"Me?"

"Yes, the Lord moves in mysterious ways. I feel that I can breathe now, that a great weight has been lifted.

"That's nice to hear."

The two women stood as a pleasant evening air rolled in, neither of them speaking.

Sr. Monica eventually broke this peaceful hush. "Can I show you something?" she asked politely.

"Of course you can."

"A little secret of mine. You mustn't tell."

"I wouldn't dream of it."

Sr. Monica took a piece of white linen from deep inside her habit. She unfolded it with great care and lay it on the palm of her hand for Helen to view. "You can take if you want."

Helen took the fabric cautiously and examined it. "A lock of hair," she said in wonderment.

"Mine, I've kept it against their will."

"Why?"

"At La Carthusian, they cut off our hair for Jesus. Sometimes I take it out to remind me of who I was."

Helen returned the linen to Sr. Monica gingerly and watched her as she refolded it with affection and replaced it inside her habit.

"A childish idea, I know," Sr. Monica said distantly.

"I don't think so."

"Can you do something else for me?"

"Anything at all, just ask."

With that, Sr. Monica took two envelopes from her habit and held one out for Helen. "Can you get this to my father?"

"Certainly."

"It explains everything, like you said."

"I'm so glad," Helen said, taking the envelope. "It will make you feel a whole lot better," she added genuinely.

"I do."

"And do you want me to say anything else?"

"That I am looking forward to seeing him, soon."

Sr. Monica then handed the second envelope to Helen. "And this is for John."

"I won't let you down," Helen said optimistically.

"That gentle nudge to help him move on." Sr. Monica said quietly.

"Is that all?"

"Yes, it's all in there."

"And I have a little secret," Helen revealed as she put the two envelopes away for safe keeping. "I met a boy."

"The French lad working on the roof," Sr. Monica declared.

Helen was taken aback. "You know."

"We sisters have our ways," Sr. Monica explained brightly with a sweep of her hands

"And we were together, last night."

"And how do you feel about that, today?" Sr. Monica asked, her tone was non-judgemental.

"Good, guilty…I dunno." Helen shrugged.

"Do you love this boy?"

"Not love. Is that a mortal sin, sister?"

"When I arrived here first my mother asked *La Mere Superieure* that if I ran away would it be a mortal sin."

"What did she say?"

"She told my mother that she could ask Jesus that herself when she met him."

"But what does that mean? Helen continued her face filled with bemusement. Sr. Monica paused to gather her thoughts before answering.

"For me, not to spend your life worrying and wondering," she offered eventually.

"Go with the flow."

"Living your life, child. May I give you one final blessing?"

"Yes, if you think it will do some good."

"It won't do any harm."

Helen bowed her head before Sr. Monica allowing her to place both her palms gently on Helen. Helen stood motionless as she received the silent blessing. Sr. Monica stepped back then and made a sign of the cross. The two women embraced spontaneously.

"I will deliver those letters for you," Helen said as they drew back from each other.

"Thank you."

"I'm glad I met you, Linda."

"The girl who ran away to be a nun!" Sr. Monica quipped.

Helen gave a jaunty wave and strolled casually across the rooftop for one final time. As Sr. Monica returned the wave, she felt content that her faith in the power of prayer and its ability to help people had been renewed. She was prepared to rededicate herself to that calling with even more fervour in the coming weeks and months ahead because that worked best when you accepted who you were yourself first. She was comfortable in her own skin again.

She crossed to the handrail and there she read the fresh hand carving. When she had finished reading, she removed the linen from her pocket one more time. She unfolded it slowly and then shook the strands of hair free into the summer night. Watching them being swept away in the wind, she crumpled up the lined fabric and thrust it back into the pocket of her habit. She rested her palms on the handrail once more with her head bowed:

L&H

Trentiemme du Julliet, dix-neuf soixante-douze

She knelt in prayer.

About the Author

If you benefited from this book, please consider posting an online review. Thank you in advance.

Derek O'Gorman is a teacher in Cork City where he lives with his wife Deirdre. Derek's first collection of short stories *Barred* was published in 2023. Derek has also written successfully for stage and among his awards are; The VSA Playwright Award, and The All-Ireland One-Act Play Award on two occasions. His work has been produced on RTE Radio and adapted for film for the Cork Midsummer Festival. Derek is also a Head Coach at UCC Soccer Club.

X: https://x.com/OgormanDerek

About the Publisher

Sulis International Press publishes select fiction and nonfiction in a variety of genres under four imprints:

- Riversong Books (fiction)

- Sulis Press (general nonfiction)

- Keledei Publications (spirituality)

- Sulis Academic Press (academic works)

For more, visit the website
https://sulisinternational.com

Subscribe to the newsletter
https://sulisinternational.com/subscribe/

Follow on social media
https://www.facebook.com/SulisInternational
https://twitter.com/Sulis_Intl
https://www.pinterest.com/Sulis_Intl/
https://www.instagram.com/sulis_international/